CALIFORNIA GIRLS!

We didn't find out until the next day that we had won ten thousand dollars — one-thousand-four hundred-and-twenty-eight dollars and about fifty-seven cents each.

"You know what?" I said, when my friends and I were actually holding the cheque. "We've got two weeks off school next month. We could use this money for a trip to California to visit my dad."

"Ooh, California," said Mallory dreamily.

So we checked with our parents, and we checked with my dad, and everything was settled. He said that my brother, Jeff, and my California friends would be on holiday then, too, and that he would try to take a week off from work.

So it was all set.

California, here we come!

The Babysitters can't believe it! They've won so much money in the Connecticut lottery that they can afford to go on holiday with Dawn to California. How can they *ever* go back to Stoneybrook, now that they're real California girls?

Also in the Babysitters Club series:

Look out for:

Babysitter Specials:

Look out for:

CALIFORNIA GIRLS!

Ann M. Martin

Hippo Books
Scholastic Publications Limited
London

Scholastic Children's Books
Scholastic Publications Ltd,
7–9 Pratt Street, London NW1 0AE, UK

Scholastic Inc.,
730 Broadway, New York, NY 10003, USA

Scholastic Canada Ltd,
123 Newkirk Road, Richmond Hill,
Ontario, Canada L4C 3G5

Ashton Scholastic Pty Ltd,
P O Box 579, Gosford, New South Wales,
Australia

Ashton Scholastic Ltd,
Private Bag 1, Penrose, Auckland,
New Zealand

First published in the US by Scholastic Inc., 1990
First published in the UK by Scholastic Publications Ltd, 1992

Copyright © 1990 Ann M Martin

ISBN 0 590 55038 1

THE BABY-SITTERS CLUB is a trademark of Scholastic Inc.

Typeset in Plantin by Contour Typesetters, Southall, London
Printed by Cox & Wyman Ltd, Reading, Berks

10 9 8 7 6 5 4 3 2 1

*This book is in memory of
Lisa Novak
and
Gregg Peretz,
whose short lives touched hundreds of others'
in unique and wonderful ways.*

They will always be remembered.

PROLOGUE

The Jack-O'-Lottery Jackpot

It all started when our state's Jack-O'-Lottery jackpot climbed to 23 million dollars. Can you believe it? *Twenty-three million.* I didn't know there was that much money in the whole world, let alone in Connecticut.

My friend Claudia had been giving her father money to buy her a lottery ticket each week for ages (kids can't buy the tickets themselves, which is incredibly unfair), but she'd never won anything, so my other friends and I were always teasing her. But when the jackpot reached 23 million dollars, the seven of us—Mary Anne Spier, Kristy Thomas, Jessi Ramsey, Stacey McGill, Mallory Pike, Claudia Kishi, and me, Dawn Schafer—chipped in enough money to buy seven tickets. We asked my mum to get the tickets

1

for us, and we agreed that if any of the tickets was a winner, we would split the money seven ways, which would be over three million dollars each. At that rate, we decided we could be women of leisure all our lives.

So anyway, on the day of the draw, we gave my mum our money and she bought us seven tickets. It was a Friday. The winning number would be drawn that night. With seven tickets, we were so sure we were going to win that we all spent the night at my house just to watch the news. Promptly at 9:59 we gathered in front of the TV for the *Ten O'Clock Report*. The Jack-O'Lottery drawing wasn't held until 10:25 and I can't say we were very patient. At one point, Kristy actually said, "Oh, who *cares* about world peace? When are they going to announce the winning ticket?"

Anyway, the newsreader finally got around to the jackpot. "And the winning number is . . . fifty-three . . ."

"*Yes!*" I shouted, looking at the ticket I was holding.

"Twenty-seven . . . thirteen . . . eight . . . seventy-one . . ."

"Yes, yes, *yes*, YES!" I couldn't believe it.

"Are you kidding, Dawn?" asked Mary Anne, who's my stepsister.

"Shh. No."

"And the final number," said the announcer, "is eleven."

"Eleven?" I cried. "No, it isn't. It's thirty-five." I almost burst into tears.

"Wait a sec," said Claud. "Has your ticket got five of the six winning numbers?"

"Yes," I replied.

"Then we've won a prize!"

We didn't find out until the next day that we had won ten thousand dollars—one-thousand-four hundred-and-twenty-eight dollars and about fifty-seven cents each.

"You know what?" I said, when my friends and I were actually holding the cheque. "We've got two weeks off school next month. We could use this money for a trip to California to visit my dad."

"Ooh, California," said Mallory dreamily.

So we checked with our parents, and we checked with my dad, and everything was settled. He said that my brother, Jeff, and my California friends would be on holiday then, too, and that he would try to take a week off from work.

So it was all set.

California, here we come!

1st CHAPTER

Dawn

"Come *on*, Mary Anne!" I cried. "We're going to be late."

"Okay, okay." My stepsister came thundering down the stairs in our house, and we ran into the garage and hopped onto our bikes. We were on our way to a meeting of the Babysitters Club at Claudia's house.

"What were you doing up there?" I asked Mary Anne as we sped along.

"Packing," she replied.

"Packing? For California?"

"*Yes*," said Mary Anne defensively.

"But we aren't leaving for another week."

"I don't want to forget anything." Mary Anne set her mouth in a firm line and I knew better than to tease her any more.

When we reached Claud's house, Mary Anne and I rode our bikes right into the Kishis' garage. (We didn't want them to get stolen, but we didn't have time to chain them to anything.) Then we raced to Claudia's bedroom, which is the headquarters for the Babysitters Club, or the BSC.

What is the BSC? Well, it's a business that my six friends and I run. It was Kristy's idea. She thought it up at the beginning of seventh grade. (Kristy, Stacey, Mary Anne, Claudia, and I are all thirteen now, and in the eighth grade. Mallory and Jessi are eleven and in the sixth grade. We go to Stoneybrook Middle School.) Anyway, Kristy's idea was for a group of her friends who babysit to get together several times a week and hold meetings. People who needed sitters could phone us during the meetings. Since they would reach several sitters, they'd almost be guaranteed to find somebody available—instead of making call after call to sitters who might not be at home.

Well, the club was a success from the beginning. It started with just four girls, and now there are the seven of us, plus two associate members. (The associate members don't come to meetings, but they are reliable sitters whom we can call on for help if a job comes in that none of us can take. Guess who the associate members are—a friend of Kristy's named Shannon Kilbourne . . . and Logan Bruno, who is Mary Anne's boyfriend!)

Anyway, the club is run very efficiently, and I

5

think that's one reason it's such a big success. Kristy runs the club because she's the chairman. And she's the chairman because the club was her idea in the first place, and also because she's always getting more good ideas for the club. She makes us keep a notebook in which we write up our babysitting experiences, and she thinks up ways to advertise the club so that we get more clients.

Kristy comes from an interesting family. There's her mum; her stepfather, Watson (her real father walked out on her family when Kristy was about six); her two older brothers, Charlie and Sam; her little brother, David Michael; her stepbrother and stepsister, Andrew and Karen, who are four and seven; her grandmother, Nannie; and her adopted sister, Emily Michelle. Emily is two-and-a-half. She came from Vietnam. Kristy and her happy, jumbled-up family live in a mansion in a different part of Stoneybrook from where the rest of us live (Karen and Andrew only live there some of the time; they live mainly with their mother and stepfather). The mansion is Watson's. It's his family home and he grew up there. But Kristy has only lived there since the summer before eighth grade. That's when her mum and Watson got married. Before that, she lived next door to Mary Anne (who's her best friend) and opposite Claud. Kristy is a tomboy and has a bit of a big mouth.

Claudia Kishi is the club vice-chairman. This is because we hold our meetings in her room, so three times a week we use her phone (Claud has not only her own phone, but a *private* phone number) and eat the junk food that she hides in her room.

Claud has a pretty ordinary family. She lives with her mum and dad and her older sister, Janine, who is a genius. Living with a genius probably isn't easy for anyone, but it's especially hard for Claudia, who is bright, but a poor pupil and an especially poor speller. Claud thinks she isn't clever, but that's not true. She just doesn't like school. What she does like is art—and she's great at it. She also likes to read Nancy Drew mysteries (but that's about the only thing she likes to read), and to eat junk food. Unlike Kristy, who is just average-looking and doesn't care much about clothes, Claudia is absolutely gorgeous and wears wild clothes. The Kishis are Japanese-American, so Claud has long, silky black hair; a complexion that somehow remains perfect, despite her junk-food addiction; and dark, almond-shaped eyes. You never know what kind of outfit or hairdo you'll see on Claud. For instance, on the day of this meeting, she was wearing a red shirt with Mexican hats and cactus plants printed on it, and blue-and-white-striped trousers held up by polka-dotted braces. On her head was what looked like an engineer's cap (it matched her trousers), and dangling from her ears were miniature cowboy boots, which she'd made herself.

Stacey McGill is the club treasurer and also Claud's best friend. Stacey is a newcomer to Stoneybrook, unlike Claud, Kristy, Mary Anne, and Mallory, who were born and grew up here. Stacey grew up in New York City but moved to Connecticut at the beginning of seventh grade. (She was one of the four original members of the BSC.) As treasurer, Stacey's job is to collect our club subs every Monday and to use the money to pay for our expenses—for instance, to help pay Claud's phone bill.

Stacey is great. She's funny, she's nice, she's *excellent* at maths (that's why she's our treasurer), and she's extremely sophisticated. That probably comes from growing up in New York, but I'm not sure. Anyway, Stacey is very mature, and she's allowed to get her blonde hair permed and to wear nail polish (usually it's sparkly) and make-up and things. And her clothes are about as wild as Claudia's. On this particular day, Stacey was wearing wide-legged, cropped trousers; her Hard Rock Cafe T-shirt; and high-topped trainers. I feel sorry for Stacey, though, because she's been through a rough time lately. Her parents have just divorced, and now her father lives in New York, and Stacey and her mum live here in Stoneybrook. As if that weren't bad enough, Stacey has a severe form of a disease called diabetes. Diabetic people have a problem with a gland in their body called the pancreas. Ordinarily, the pancreas makes something called insulin, which breaks down the sugar in your body. But when that doesn't happen properly, you develop diabetes and have to work out other ways to control your blood-sugar level. Some people can do that through diet alone—by watching how many sweets they eat. But poor Stacey not only has to be on a *strictly* controlled diet (including calorie-counting), she has to give herself injections of insulin every day. I don't know how she does that. *I* couldn't do it, so I really admire Stacey.

The BSC secretary is Mary Anne Spier, who, as I said before, is also my stepsister. (I'll explain how that happened in just a minute.) Mary Anne's job is one of the biggest (certainly the busiest) of the whole club. It's up to her to keep our record book in order. That's where we keep track of our clients—their names, addresses, phone numbers, and the rates they pay. More important, it's up to Mary Anne to arrange every single job that comes in. That means she has to know all our timetables—when Claud has art classes, when Stacey will be in New York visiting her father, etc. But Mary Anne is super-organized, so she's terrific at this job.

Now—I'll explain how Mary Anne, from

Connecticut, and I, Dawn Schafer from California, came to be stepsisters. It started when my mum and dad got divorced. (I could sympathize with Stacey when she was going through *her* parents' divorce.) My family—Mum, Dad, my younger brother, Jeff, and I—were living in California then, but after my parents' split, Mum moved Jeff and me to Stoneybrook because she'd grown up here. Jeff and I weren't too happy about the move. In fact, Jeff never adjusted to life here, which is how he ended up back in California with Dad. I made friends straight away, though, and the first one was Mary Anne. It's sort of a long story, but we found out that Mary Anne's dad and my mum had gone out together when they were at high school. So we got them together again and they began dating. (Oh, I suppose it's important to mention that Mr Spier was a widower; Mrs Spier died when Mary Anne was really little.) Anyway, after they'd dated for what seemed like forever, my mum and Mr Spier got married, and Mary Anne, her dad, and her kitten, Tigger, all moved into my house. Mary Anne and I are glad to be stepsisters as well as friends, even though we're very different people. For one thing, we look different. Mary Anne has brown hair and brown eyes, and is short, just like Kristy. I have *long* blonde hair and blue eyes (People tell me I look like a California girl, whatever that means), and I dress in my own style. I'm an individual and pretty independent. Mary Anne, on the other hand, is quiet, shy, a romantic, and much more conservative than I am. (I have two holes pierced in each ear, and Mary Anne has no holes. Sometimes she acts as though I'm a barbarian or something.) But Mary Anne and I get along very well most of the time. After all, she's my best friend.

Let's see. In the BSC, I hold the position of alternative officer. I'm a bit like a substitute teacher or an understudy in a play. In other words, I take over the duties of anyone who might have to miss a meeting, so I have to know what everyone does. But the club members rarely miss meetings, so mostly I answer the phone a lot.

Jessi Ramsey and Mallory Pike are our junior officers. This is because they are eleven and not allowed to babysit at night unless they're watching their own brothers and sisters. They're a big help to the rest of us, though, since they take on so many after-school and weekend jobs.

Jessi and Mal are also best friends, even though (like Mary Anne and me) they are pretty different people. Well, they do have some things in common. They both love children (of course); they both love to read, especially horse stories; and they're the oldest kids in their families, yet they feel that their parents treat them like babies. However, Jessi is a talented (*really* talented) dancer who might want to be a professional

11

ballerina one day, while Mal loves to write and draw and is thinking of becoming a children's author and illustrator. Then, while Jessi has a pretty ordinary family—she lives with her parents; her Aunt Cecelia; her younger sister, Becca; and her baby brother, Squirt—Mallory has *seven* brothers and sisters. And three of them—Adam, Jordan, and Byron—are identical triplets. The others are named Vanessa, Nicky, Margo, and Claire. Claire is the baby. One final difference between Jessi and Mal is that Jessi is black and Mal is white.

Okay, so that's the BSC.

When Mary Anne and I raced into Claud's room for the meeting that afternoon, we found that we were the last to arrive.

"Mary Anne was packing for California," I couldn't help saying.

Mary Anne glared at me, but everyone else laughed.

Then Kristy called the meeting to order, and we tried to be businesslike and professional for the next half hour, but it was hard. We were too excited about California.

"You won't believe all the things we can do there," I said. "In L.A. alone there are a million things."

"You mean besides Disneyland?" asked Mal.

"Definitely," I replied. "We'll probably drive to Hollywood—"

"*Hollywood*?!" shrieked my stepsister. (She gets absolutely gooey over big cities and film stars and things.)

At this point, Claud couldn't help getting a little dig in. "And you all thought I was stupid buying lottery tickets all this time," she said. She looked pretty smug.

"Well, not *stupid*," said Stacey. "Just, um, frivolous."

"I'm not sure what *frivolous* means," replied Claud, "but whatever it is, it paid off. We've got plane tickets and plenty of spending money."

"And I'll get to see my dad and Jeff," I added.

"Oh, my lord!" said Claudia. "How are we going to wait until next Saturday?"

Saturday

Dear Becca and Squirt,

Hi! you two! Well, here I am on the plane to California. If my writing looks funny, it's because the ride is a little bumpy. That's due to turbulense, which scares Mary Anne to death, but I'm not too nervous. So far, we have had lunch. Soon, they're going to show a film. I am so, so excited!

Love from
Jessi

Rebecca Ramsey and
John Philip Ramsey, Jr.
612 Fawcett Avenue

Stoneybrook, Ct. 06800

2nd CHAPTER

Jessi

I don't think you can imagine a more excited group of travellers than my friends and I. You'd think we were on our way to Paris or somewhere exotic. Well, actually, California *is* exotic, as far as I'm concerned.

Anyway, we boarded our plane, and it turned out to be *huge*. There were nine seats across— two, then an aisle, five, then another aisle, and two more. My friends and I were seated in two of the seats on the left-hand side of the plane and a row of those five middle seats. Needless to say, there was some clambering over who got the window seat, but in the end, Stacey pointed out that Claudia's boarding pass placed her by the window, so Claud took the seat happily. (She also offered to swap places with us now and then so we could each have a turn at the window.)

"Put on your seat belts, everybody," said Mary Anne nervously.

But we couldn't. Not straight away. We were too busy getting settled. We put our jackets in the overhead lockers. Then Dawn said, "This plane is *freezing*," and took her jacket *out* of the locker, along with a blanket. Then Mary Anne and Claudia wanted pillows, and Stacey remembered that she'd put her boarding pass in her jacket pocket, so *she* had to get her jacket, too. When we were finally seated, Mary Anne reminded us to fasten our seat belts again.

We all did except for Kristy, who wasn't paying any attention.

"Why is it," Kristy began, "that all planes smell the same? Sort of like coffee . . . and I don't know, um—"

"Is this going to be disgusting?" Mary Anne asked her. And before Kristy had time to answer, Mary Anne added, "Fasten your seat belt."

This time Kristy did.

"Who wants to play hangman?" asked Mallory.

"You're not bored already, are you?" I said. "Because this flight is over five hours long. Maybe we should save hangman for later."

"Hey, look!" exclaimed Stacey. "We're going to get a film on this trip. There's the screen. I wonder what we're going to see."

"It's an old classic," said an air hostess who

happened to be passing. "I hope you like Alfred Hitchcock. We're showing Hitchcock films this month. Today's is called *Vertigo*."

"Thanks," said Stacey as the air hostess passed by.

"Who's Alfred Hitchcock?" asked Mallory.

"Who's Vertigo?" asked Claud.

But at that moment, the plane roared to life.

"Ooh," said Mary Anne, gripping the arms of her seat. "I'm glad I'm where I am." (She was in the middle of the five seats, between Kristy and me.) "Hey, Claudia," she called, "you don't have to share your seat with me."

"Are you afraid of flying?" I asked Mary Anne.

"No. I'm afraid of crashing."

I couldn't help giggling.

Soon the plane was taxiing down the runway. "Cabin crew please prepare for takeoff," said the pilot's voice over the loudspeaker. And a few seconds later, the plane rose gently above the ground and began to soar higher and higher. I tried to look out of the windows, but all I could see was sky. Claudia must have been able to see something, though, because she was craning her neck around, gazing at whatever was below us.

"Hangman?" Mal asked again.

"Maybe after lunch," I replied.

We soon reached "cruising altitude", the seat belt sign was turned off, and the air hostesses began coming down the aisles with the trolleys of lunch trays.

"Today we have a choice of chicken or spaghetti," said an air hostess, leaning over so that Dawn, Mary Anne, Kristy, Mal, and I could hear her. "What'll it be?"

"Spaghetti," said everyone except Dawn, who chose the chicken. (Across the aisle, Stacey also asked for the chicken. But Claud asked for spaghetti. She absolutely loves it.)

Plastic trays were set in front of us. Everything was in little compartments, like a TV dinner. And the forks and knives and things were packed in plastic.

"This must be so that things won't slide around in case there's a sudden drop in cabin pressure and the plane takes a nosedive," said Mary Anne.

"I don't know," I replied. "In first class, the passengers eat on china plates, and their silverware comes rolled up in linen napkins."

"*Really*?" said Mary Anne. "Gosh, I wish we'd had enough money for first-class seats. That would have been so cool."

We began our meal. The food was like school cafeteria food. But it was more fun to eat. And our conversation was *definitely* more interesting. We had California on the brain.

"You know where I want to go when we get to L.A.?" Claudia shouted to Dawn. (I'm sure the other passengers loved us.)

19

"Where?" asked Dawn.

"To Knott's Berry Farm."

"A *berry* farm?" I exclaimed. Gosh. You could go to berry farms in Connecticut.

"No, *Knott's* Berry Farm," said Dawn. "It's an amusement park."

"Oh. Then I want to go there, too," I replied. "And I want to go to Hollywood. I want to see that wax museum."

"You want to go to Hollywood just to see the museum?" asked Mal. "What about seeing the homes of film stars? Now *that's* why people go to Hollywood."

"Is there a sports hall of fame in L.A.?" Kristy wondered.

Dawn frowned. "If there is, I don't know about it. Ask Jeff when we get to California. He'll know. Or my dad will know."

"I want to go to Grauman's Chinese Theatre," said Stacey.

"Yeah! Just like they did in *I Love Lucy*," agreed Claud. "Only we won't try to steal John Wayne's footprints."

I had no idea what Claud was talking about, and I didn't want to ask. But I did say, "Hey, Dawn, can we go to the San Diego Zoo? I've always wanted to go there. It's supposed to be one of the best zoos—"

"Jessi," interrupted Dawn. "Go to San Diego? Do you know how far that is from Los Angeles?

California's a big state," she reminded me.

"We *are* going to Hollywood, though," said Mary Anne. We had finished eating, and one of the air hostesses had cleared our food away. Mary Anne had left her tray down, though, and now it was covered with about a million maps, as well as pamphlets about California.

"Where'd you get all that stuff?" Dawn asked Mary Anne.

"From a travel agent. Listen, you wouldn't *believe* what we can do in Hollywood. I mean, we can look at the stars' homes and go to Grauman's and the wax museum, but there's also the Universal Studios tour and the Walk of Fame. Oh, and we can go to Beverly Hills, too, can't we? Because there are tons of stars' homes *there*. You know, we can buy maps that show us where the different homes are. And if you really want to go to a zoo, Jessi, there's one in L.A. As well as lots of gardens and museums. And let's see. Near Hollywood, there are these prehistoric fossil pits. Oh, Kristy, you might want to see the Rose Bowl Stadium."

Mary Anne would probably have gone on talking forever, except that the lights in the cabin were dimmed, and the film began. All seven of us had hired headphones earlier, so for the next couple of hours we sat in dead silence, watching this really scary film.

When the film ended, the air hostesses brought

21

Jessi

the drinks trolleys around and we all got free
mineral water and orange juice. And peanuts.
After that, I fell asleep and didn't wake up until
we were getting ready to land. As the plane
skimmed along the runway, Mary Anne gripped
the arms of her seat so tightly her knuckles turned
white. But the landing was perfect, and before we
knew it, we had collected our things out of the
luggage compartments, filed off the plane, and
were entering the airport, when Dawn shouted,
"Dad! Jeff! Here we are!"

Rushing towards us were Jeff (whom I've met
several times) and Mr Schafer (whom I've never
met). Actually, I don't think any of Dawn's
friends has met him. But he was really nice.
Patient, too. We had to wait for about forty-five
minutes to claim our luggage. (This is partly
because Stacey and Claudia had packed so much.)
And then he put up with a pretty long drive in a
borrowed van to Dawn's house with the seven of
us, plus Jeff, giggling and talking loudly the
whole way.

"I can't believe we're in California," I said, as
we drove along. "Warm weather, palm trees . . ."

"Gorgeous boys," added Claudia.

"Film stars," added Mary Anne, which
reminded me of something.

"Hey, I've got to ring Derek Masters tonight,"
I said.

Derek is an eight-year-old boy whose family is

22

from Stoneybrook, and who I've babysat for. But guess what? He's not any ordinary everyday child. He's one of the stars of a TV comedy series called *P.S. 162*, which is filmed in L.A. So he and his family live out here while Derek is filming. He and I have kept in touch, and I promised him I'd phone when I got to California.

When we finally reached Dawn's house, two things happened—one bad and one good. The bad thing was that Dawn found Carol, her father's girlfriend, waiting for us. Carol had come over and was cooking that night's dinner. Dawn was *not* pleased. The good thing was that I contacted Derek's mum (Derek was at the studio) and she invited me to watch Derek film on Wednesday. Mr Schafer said I could go. I couldn't believe I would actually be able to visit the set of *P.S. 162*. My holiday was off to an incredible start!

Sunday

Dear Mom, Watson, Nannie, Charlie, Sam, David Michael, and Emily,

Well, I've used up half this card just writing your names! Okay, so here we are in California. We got here safe and sound yesterday. Dawn's house is really nice. So is her father. There's plenty of things to do around here, but we're quite jet-lagged so we didn't make any plans today. However, we are going to meet the members of the We ♥ Kids Club.

Lots of Love,
Kristy

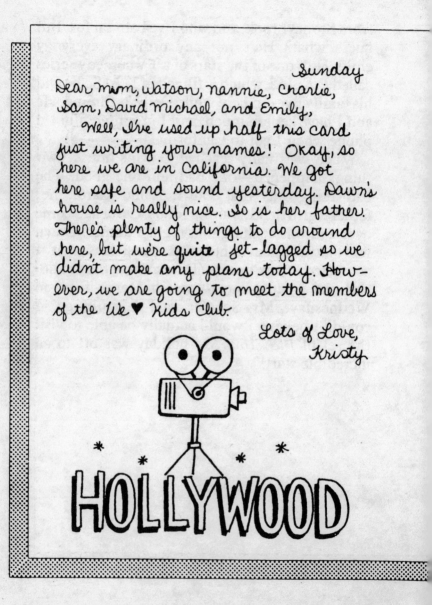

HOLLYWOOD

The Brewer and Thomas Family

1210 McLelland Road

Stoneybrook, Ct. 06800

3rd
CHAPTER

Kristy

Gosh, that three-hour time change really makes a difference! I didn't think it would, but it did. What happened was that our flight took off at about midday. Then we flew for five hours or so, but when we got to California, it was only about two o'clock on the West Coast. It *felt* like five o'clock to my friends and me, though. And when we went to bed at ten-thirty that night, it felt like one-thirty to our poor, confused bodies.

So we slept later than we meant to the next morning, and were all a bit groggy for a while after we got up. Even Dawn, who felt that, as our hostess, she should ask us what we wanted to do that day. Luckily, none of us said anything.

"So you don't mind just hanging around today?" she asked.

"Not one bit," said Mary Anne.

In all honesty, I wanted to go back to bed, but since so many of us were visiting the Schafers, my bed was a sleeping bag on the floor of Dawn's room. And I was *not* tired enough to want to go back to the sleeping bag.

Anyway, things started to get interesting straight away.

You see, Mr Schafer hired a housekeeper to cook and clean for him and Jeff. Her name is Mrs Bruen, and Dawn has met her and likes her. But she doesn't come on Sundays. However, Carol arrived in time to help Mr Schafer make brunch. Immediately, I could see Dawn's hackles go up. I couldn't work out why. Carol seemed nice enough. She likes music, and knows a lot about MTV and music videos and things.

But Dawn acted as though brunch couldn't be over fast enough for her. In fact, when the phone rang just as everyone was finishing, Dawn made a beeline for it. I heard her say, "Hello?" There was a pause. Then Dawn cried, "Sunny!"

Sunny Winslow is Dawn's best friend in California. She and two of her friends have started their own babysitting club. It's called the We ♥ Kids Club, and it's based on the BSC. (When Dawn first moved to Stoneybrook, she wrote to Sunny so often and told her so much about the BSC that Sunny just couldn't resist starting a California sitting business.)

27

A few minutes later, I heard Dawn put down the phone. She ran back to the patio, where we were eating. "Guess what, you lot? Sunny's invited us over today. Does the BSC want to meet the We ♥ Kids Club?"

I was the first to answer. "Definitely," I said. I'd been dying to see how another club runs. So Dawn called Sunny back and told her we'd come over around midday.

"I'd better warn you about something," Dawn was saying.

It was 12:15, and Dawn, Claudia, Jessi, Mal, Stacey, Mary Anne, and I were standing at the Winslows' front door. Sunny's house looked a lot like Dawn's—skylights in the roof, sprawling and modern. But it was a two-storey house, and Dawn's is all on one level.

"Warn us? About what?" I asked.

"The We ♥ Kids Club doesn't work exactly the same way our club does. Sunny and Jill and Maggie are sort of, oh, relaxed about things."

"Do they get as many jobs as we do?" I asked.

Dawn shrugged. "Probably not. There are only three of them, and there are seven of us, plus Logan and Shannon."

I didn't say anything. I was already beginning to feel . . . funny. I knew there was no reason to be competitive, but, well, I *did* feel that I had sort of invented babysitting clubs, and that I knew

28

best. I told myself to calm down, though. I didn't want to get off on the wrong foot with Dawn's friends.

Dawn rang the Winslows' bell and a moment later, the door flew open. A grinning girl ran out, and she and Dawn hugged and hugged. Then Sunny said, "Come on upstairs. Jill and Maggie are here."

We followed Sunny to her bedroom. Sitting on her floor were two girls. They stood up when they saw us, and then the introductions began. Sunny said, "Members of the BSC, meet the We Love Kids Club. I'm Sunny Winslow. This is Maggie Blume, and this is Jill Henderson."

Then Dawn introduced the BSC to Sunny, Maggie and Jill. Phew!

The ten of us crowded on to the floor and Sunny's bed.

"Where does the chairman sit?" I asked Sunny.

"Chairman?" she repeated. "Oh, we don't have officers in our club."

"You don't? But how do you know who should do which jobs?"

"We just do whatever needs doing," Sunny replied. She sounded a little testy.

"How often do you read your club notebook?" I couldn't help asking. I was pretty sure there was no notebook. (I was right.)

"We've got an appointment book, though," said Jill. "And we made Kid-Kits like yours."

"We-ell . . ." Now I felt flattered.

I felt even more flattered when Maggie said, "Kristy, I was wondering. You're chairman of your club and you thought it up, right?" (I nodded.) "So what do you do if nobody can take a job that comes in?"

I was in the middle of explaining about our associate members when Sunny's phone rang. She picked it up. "Hello?" she said. "Oh, hi, Mr Robertson . . . Wednesday afternoon? Let me check. Hold on." Sunny cupped her hand over the mouthpiece. "Can anyone sit for Stephie on Wednesday?"

Maggie and Jill shook their heads.

"Too bad. I can't, either," said Sunny. She took her hand off the receiver, then immediately put it back. "Hey, do any of *you* lot want a sitting job?" Obviously, she meant the members of the BSC.

"For Stephie Robertson?" said Dawn. "I remember her. She's really sweet. She lives with just her father, doesn't she? No mum or brothers or sisters."

"Right," answered Sunny.

"You know," said Dawn, "Mary Anne, I bet you'd be perfect for Stephie. You two have a lot in common."

Well, by this time, my mouth must have looked like the entrance to the Lincoln Tunnel. That's how wide it was open. I couldn't believe what had just happened. As soon as Sunny got off the phone, having told Mr Robertson that a good friend of Dawn Schafer's could sit for his daughter, I exclaimed, "What's going on here?"

"What do you mean?" asked Sunny.

"Well, is this the way you always conduct meetings? And why are people calling you on a Sunday? Do you have meetings on Sundays?"

"Oh, no. We hold our meetings after school. Usually two or three times a week for half an hour or so."

"Two *or* three times a week? For half an hour *or* so? You mean you don't have regular meetings? Is that why people are calling on Sunday?"

"Of course," replied Maggie. "They can call whenever they want."

"Do they always call here?"

"No, they can call at any of our houses."

Hmmph. This was a sorry excuse for a baby-sitting club.

I just had to ask one more question. "How do you decide who gets the jobs that come in during meetings?"

"Oh, we take whatever we want," said Jill. (I decided not to ask why they even bothered with an appointment book.)

"Listen, Mary Anne," said Sunny. "There's something you should know about Stephie. She's asthmatic."

Dawn clapped her hand to her forehead.

"That's right! How could I have forgotten? Yes, Mary Anne. Stephie has asthma. I learned about it when I used to sit for her."

Mary Anne looked alarmed, so Jill said, "Don't worry. Stephie's been living with it for a long time. She's got an inhaler and knows how to use it. She's got pills, too."

"Wait!" cried Mallory. "What's asthma? What's an inhaler?"

"Asthma is a condition," replied Dawn, "in which a person's bronchial passages—those are the breathing tubes—close up sometimes and then the person has trouble breathing. It can be serious because a person can *stop* breathing, but that doesn't happen often. Anyway, inhalers help the breathing to start again. Stephie—or her father or whoever—always carries one. It's small. She puts it in her mouth, breathes in, and whatever is in the inhaler makes the breathing tubes open up again."

"Okay," said Mary Anne uncertainly. And Mal looked relieved that *she* wasn't going to be sitting for Stephie.

The phone rang again, and Sunny answered it. "Hello?" She didn't even say, "Hello, We ♥ Kids Club." Then again, how would she know whether this was a personal call or a business call?

It turned out to be a business call.

"Anyone want to sit for Erick and Ryan on Saturday?" asked Sunny.

It was a good thing her hand was cupped over the receiver because Jill and Maggie both groaned loudly.

"What's wrong with Erick and Ryan?" I asked.

"They're terrors, that's what," said Maggie.

"Well, I'll sit for them," I said. I would show the We ♥ Kids Club what a *real* babysitter could do.

Sunny arranged the job for me, telling Erick and Ryan's mother that I was a responsible sitter and also a good friend of Dawn Schafer's. But as soon as she hung up, she said, "Kristy, you don't know what you've got yourself into."

I didn't care. Anyway, I didn't think I'd got myself into anything. I'm an excellent sitter. I can handle all kinds of kids. But Sunny, Jill, and Maggie were bombarding me with rapid-fire advice:

"Give those boys an inch and they'll take a mile."

"Don't let them out of your sight for a *second*."

"Set down rules with them right away."

Huh! I thought. I don't have to listen to this. Especially from members of a club that doesn't have officers and doesn't even hold regular meetings. Whoever Erick and Ryan were, however tough they were, I knew I could handle them. And I would do it my own way.

Monday

Dear Mum and Richard,

Hi! How are you? It is terrific here in California, and I'm very glad to be back. (But don't worry, Mum. I'll return to Connecticut.) Today we went to the beach -- the entire BSC, Jeff, Bob (that friend of his), and... Carol. Dad's working, but he's taking next week off. More about Carol later.

Love and Sunshine,
Dawn

Mr and Mrs Richard Spier

177 Burnt Hill Road

Stoneybrook, Ct. 06800

4th CHAPTER

Dawn

On Monday, my friends and I had settled in. We were over our jet lag, and, well, it was easy to feel excited and happy, what with the beautiful weather we were having. It really was good to be back home... Uh-oh! Did I call California *home*? Well, it's hard not to think of it that way. After all, I was born and grew up there. But I had every intention of going back to Stoneybrook. Staying in California with Dad and Jeff wasn't an issue. Partly, I'm ashamed to say, that was because of Carol, at least during the first week-and-a-half of our visit.

She was at our house all the time. She was there on Saturday when my friends and I arrived from Connecticut. She came back on Sunday. At first, I thought that was just because Mrs Bruen wasn't there, and Carol wanted to help cook. But she was back *again* on Monday. She arrived not long after Mrs Bruen did.

I'm not proud to say this, but when she rang our doorbell and I answered it, I greeted Carol by saying, "What are you doing here?"

Carol, who had been smiling, continued to smile. (She smiles far, far too much.) "Hey," she said. "Your dad's got to work this week. Someone has to drive you kids around. This is your holiday."

"Mrs Bruen can drive us," I said. (I hadn't even let Carol through the door.)

"No, I can't!" called Mrs Bruen from the kitchen. "My job is here."

"And *my* job is flexible," said Carol. (She's a painter.) "I can work whenever I feel like it. So I decided to take a holiday now, too."

Great, I thought. Terrific. Fantastic.

Carol pushed past me into our house. She dropped her bag on the floor and said, "So what do you want to do today?"

"Beach!" cried Kristy, Jessi, Claudia, Stacey, Mallory, and Jeff.

"Hollywood!" cried Mary Anne.

I didn't say anything.

"The beach it is, then," said Carol. "Get your things together. I borrowed the mini-van from my friend again. You lot would never have fitted into my car." (Carol drives something small and

red. It's too young for her. But then, I thought
Carol was too young for my father.)

My friends and Jeff and I scrambled around,
putting on our swimsuits and packing beach bags
with suntan oil, books, sunglasses, visors, combs,
and a radio. Mary Anne packed more stuff than
the rest of us. She's very sensitive to the sun, so
she had to bring along a hat, barrier cream for her
nose and lips, an extra towel, and this embarrass-
ing kaftan she wears to ensure that every inch of
her body is protected from the sun.

"I hope you've got a parasol," she said to me as
we were leaving.

"I have. It's in the van," Carol spoke up.
"Chairs and tapes and three Walkmans, too."

"Great!" exclaimed Stacey. "I can tell this is
going to be a terrific day."

Fat chance, I thought. But I thanked Mrs
Bruen as she handed us a huge basket packed with
a picnic lunch. And then I followed everyone out
to the van parked in our front drive.

After stopping to pick up Jeff's friend Rob, we
were really on our way. The drive to the beach
took a while, since we don't live exactly on the
coast, but even I had to admit that it was worth it
when we arrived. As I said before, the weather
was absolutely gorgeous. And then, of course,
there was the Pacific Ocean, and a wide stretch of
bleached white sand before it. In Stoneybrook,
we actually do live on the water, but there are no

beaches like this one. I just love the California beach.

"All right!" I said as we trudged across the sand with our things, looking for the perfect spot to settle down. When we found one, Carol put up the parasol, Stacey and Claud spread out a beach blanket (it was really an old bedspread), and Mary Anne immediately gravitated towards the shade, where she plastered herself with suntan lotion that was factor eighty-five or something.

Soon we were all sitting or lying down, just enjoying the sun and the sound of the waves. But that didn't last long. Jeff and Rob became restless and ran to the sea to go swimming. Claudia sat up and began staring at something (I wasn't sure what), and Stacey sat up, too, and said, "Oh, *wow!*"

"What?" Jessi asked Stacey.

"Surfers. Look! I've always dreamed of going surfing."

"You could have a lesson today, if you want," spoke up Carol.

"Carol!" I exclaimed. "Surfing's very dangerous."

"No, it isn't," she said. "Not if you learn properly."

Stacey was already on her feet. "How do I get a lesson? Where do I go?"

"See that building down the beach?" said

Carol, pointing. "That's a surfboard hire place. And there are surfing instructors who give lessons every day. You could sign up for a beginners' class."

"Can I go now?" asked Stacey.

"Of course," replied Carol.

"Who's coming with me?" Stacey wanted to know.

"Not me," said Claud dreamily, still staring at whatever it was.

"Kristy?" asked Stacey. "You love sports."

"I know. But I've seen *Jaws* too many times."

"Don't even think about asking me," said Mary Anne, in her kaftan, hat, sunglasses, and factor eighty-five.

"Maybe I'll join you later," I said, just so that Stacey wouldn't feel bad.

"Okay." Stacey trotted down the beach.

Kristy, Jessi and Mal joined Jeff and Rob in the water. Mary Anne read a book under the umbrella, and Carol took out a pad of paper and began sketching. Claudia was still staring at something.

I nudged her. "What are you looking at?" I whispered.

Claud turned round slowly, as if she were in a dream, or as if *I* were dreaming. "I'm looking at that boy," she replied in a low voice.

"What boy?" The beach was getting crowded. There were boys everywhere.

41

"The one right over there." Claud tried to point without being obvious.

"Reading the book?" I asked.

"Yes."

"Why are you staring at him?"

"Why? *Why*? Because he's the most gorgeous guy I've ever seen."

Claud continued to stare. The boy *was* good-looking. Jet-black hair, dark eyes like Claud's and a serious, handsome face. He was about her age, and he was sitting all alone, reading a thick book.

"I wish I could see what he's reading," said Claud.

"Why don't you go and ask him?" said Carol, still sketching away. "Go and introduce yourself to him."

What a nerve!

But Claudia said, "Well, maybe I will . . . later."

Jessi and Mal came back from the sea, dripping. As they dried themselves, Mal exclaimed, "Hey, there's Stacey!"

Sure enough, a small class of surfers was paddling out into the water. A wave was approaching them. Claudia turned around just in time to see this.

"Oh, my lord!" she cried.

But the surfboards just rose and fell as the wave swelled under them.

Stacey's class lasted for about an hour. Even

from way down the beach, I could tell that Stacey was having the time of her life. And before the class was over, she had actually tried to ride her first wave in—shakily—and she'd fallen off before the end of her ride. But she'd come up grinning. Stacey was in love with surfing.

"Uh-oh," I said. "She's got it."

"Who's got what?" asked Mary Anne.

"Stacey's got the surfing bug."

When Stacey returned to us, she was brimming over with the joys of surfing. As we unpacked our picnic lunch, she told us everything. "I felt powerful," she said.

"Claudia," whispered Carol. "How about inviting that boy over for lunch? He's been sitting by himself all morning."

"Well . . . okay." Claud agreed so quickly, I knew she'd been thinking about doing that anyway.

I watched her get up, walk over to the boy, and speak to him briefly. The next thing I knew, he was sitting on our blanket with us. His name was Terry.

We found out a lot about Terry while we ate lunch. He lived not far away, sort of between the beach and my house. He had two brothers, one older and one younger. Both of his parents were lawyers. Then we started talking about school. Terry loved it. He was taking advanced classes, his hobby was reading, and he had recently won first prize in a district-wide science competition.

I watched Claudia blanch when she heard all that. I could almost see her thinking. This boy's not for me. But Terry seemed *very* interested in Claud.

When lunch was over, Claud carried a chair to Terry's spot in the sand, and they sat and talked. Meanwhile, Mallory, who had been gazing up and down the beach, finally announced, "Every single girl here is blonde. That's so unfair."

It wasn't true, anyhow. Jessi, Kristy, Mary Anne, and Claudia weren't blonde. And neither were a lot of other people. "I want to be a California girl, too," she said. She thought for a moment. Then she went on, "Hey! Maybe I could put some of that shampoo blonde dye in my hair!"

I waited for Carol to say, "No, that's not a good idea." But she just smiled.

I sighed. The day wore on. Everyone but Mary Anne went swimming. Claud and Terry talked some more. Mallory moaned about her hair. Also her freckles. And Stacey talked so much about surfing that when I saw some kids I used to go to school with, and remembered that they were devoted surfers, I introduced Stacey to them. They were a few years older than Stacey, but they seemed to hit it off with her right away.

44

When the day ended, I decided that it had been pleasant enough. But for some reason, I felt unsettled.

Tuesday

Dear Laine,

Well, here I am in California. How's New York? I miss you. I wish you could have come on this trip.

Yesterday I learned how to surf. Sort of. I'm just beginning. But I met some friends of Dawn's who are excellent surfers and plan to go to the beach every day of the summer. Today I'm going with them. Think of me when you think of waves♥

Luv, Stacey

Laine Cummings
The Dakota
72ND and Central Park West

New York, NY 10000

5th CHAPTER

Stacey

Straight after breakfast on Tuesday, Carol turned up again. She had the van with her. "At your service!" she said.

I saw Dawn roll her eyes. I know why she doesn't like Carol. It's because Carol acts as though she's one of us when she's really an adult.

"She tries to be such pals with us," Dawn had complained the night before. "And she's much too old for that." (Carol's about 32.) "She told Claud to invite Terry to have lunch with us, she told you about the surfing lessons, and she actually *smiled* when Mal said she wanted to dye her hair blonde."

I didn't see a thing wrong with any of this, but I kept my mouth closed. I didn't want to get into an argument with Dawn over Carol. I also didn't want to tell Dawn that *maybe* she was right about one thing. I wasn't sure I should have gone surfing yesterday. I'd been feeling a little dizzy— even though I'd been extra careful about my diet, and had remembered my insulin and everything. Oh, well. Maybe yesterday I was still just jet-lagged. Today I felt great.

And today I was going surfing again! Dawn's friends had asked me yesterday afternoon if I wanted to come to the beach with them today. I said yes straight away. I didn't think anyone else was going to the beach, and I wanted a chance to surf again. Dawn's friends had said they'd pick me up at nine-thirty in the morning.

It turned out that not only was no one else going to the beach, but everyone was splitting up. Dawn (who said she couldn't take two days in a row with Carol) announced that she wanted to ride her bike to a nearby shopping centre.

"Anyone want to come with me?" she asked.

"Of course," said Kristy.

"Why not?" said Claud.

Dawn borrowed bikes from Sunny and Jill (Jeff said he needed his bike that day), and the three of them rode off.

Mary Anne had decided to stay at home and look through more of her pamphlets and maps and books. She was acting in the same way that she did when she, Kristy, Claud and Dawn came to visit me in New York. Mary Anne could have been our tour guide then. For that matter, she could have been the tour guide for visiting foreign dignitaries. Somehow, she knew *every*thing about the city *I'd* grown up in and that she just dreamed of visiting. Now, here she was in California, doing the same thing. Oh, well. She'd be happy reading up on Forest Lawn and amusement parks and film studios.

Mal and Jessi were the only ones who chose to go off with Carol, and you won't believe where they went. Carol drove·them all the way to Hollywood just so that Mal could visit the Max Factor Museum of Beauty. No kidding! Ever since Mallory had decided that she needed to become a blonde, she hadn't talked about a thing except make-up and hair dye and beauty. Then, among Mary Anne's collection of pamphlets, she found an ad for a beauty museum, where you can see things that Max Factor, legendary make-up artist to the stars, created to enhance the beauty of Joan Crawford, Judy Garland, and lots of other actresses. You could also visit the Max Factor Boutique, where you can buy Max Factor perfume, make-up, and skin-care things, *and* talk to cosmetic experts. This was going to be a dream come true for Mallory.

At nine-fifty, my surfer friends (they weren't very punctual) slowed to a halt in front of Dawn's house in a souped-up-looking car and honked the horn, which they didn't need to do since at that point they were so late that I was plastered against the front window.

I ran out to meet them, beach gear in hand. "Hi!" I cried.

"Hi," answered Paul, who was driving. He had a sports car with the top down. (Oh, *cool*!) But Paul said, "Sorry. The doors don't work. You'll have to climb in." So I did, feeling clumsy.

Next to Paul was Alana. I squeezed into the back seat with Rosemary and Carter. Paul was seventeen. So was Carter. Rosemary and Alana were sixteen.

"Ready for another day of riding the waves?" asked Carter with a grin.

"Of course," I replied as Paul screeched off down the street so fast my head snapped back.

Whoa!

We sped to the beach and reached it fifteen minutes faster than Carol had. The ride was scary but exhilarating—and, when we walked across the sand and I saw the waves again, I felt a thrill of excitement go through me.

SURFING!

The five of us hired surfboards. (Well, actually only three of us did. I forgot to mention that Carter and Rosemary had their own boards. They had been jammed into the car with us, sticking up and over the back of the boot like big fishtails.) Then Carter and everyone went off on their own,

51

and I signed up for another surfing class. Soon I was riding the waves again.

Okay, maybe I wasn't exactly riding the waves, hanging ten, or doing any of the other things my new friends could already do. But I was getting there. I loved the feel of sitting on the board and paddling out to sea. I liked bobbing up and down, thinking of the cool green water below me, and under that, the sea bed. Later, as soon as Dan, our instructor, allowed us to, I stood up on my board. And this time I rode a wave in without falling off. In all honesty it was fun—but scary. Dan had just said, "Wait! Don't try that one. It's too big!" But for me, it was also too late. I'd stood up, the wave had carried me off, and there was nothing I could do about it. I was whizzing through a tunnel of water, and I didn't know how to stop. What if this wave just *engulfs* me? I thought, my heart pounding. My knees began to feel weak, which wasn't good, because I needed them to support me. Then, just as I was about to panic completely, the wave fizzled out and I found myself on the beach. I was really impressed with myself.

Dan wasn't, though. As soon as he rode in he said, "Stacey! What were you doing? You could have killed yourself."

"But I didn't," I said. And when the lesson was over, I rented my board for the rest of the day, and joined Alana and Carter and everyone. I wasn't nearly as good as they were, but I'd definitely got the feel of surfing, and I kept riding the waves in—big or small.

Early in the afternoon, I realized I needed to eat something, so I went to the snack bar and bought a salad. I was walking with it down the beach to my towel when I passed someone who looked familiar. It was Terry.

"Hey, Terry," I said. "It's me, Stacey. Claudia's friend."

Terry looked up. He was sitting in a chair, engrossed in the same big book he'd been reading the day before, only now he was much further into it.

"Hi!" he said. "Is Claudia here?"

"Not today," I replied. I sat down next to him and began to eat my salad. "She and Kristy and Dawn went to a shopping centre," I told him.

"Oh," said Terry, sounding disappointed.

I took that as a good sign. The night before, Claud had told me she wouldn't be seeing Terry again. "I like him a lot," she had said, "but we're not right for each other. He's much too clever for me. Going out with him would be a bit like dating a male version of Janine. What would we talk about? I don't know a thing about science, and I bet that even though he's read about a million books, none of them was a Nancy Drew." She'd paused. "Besides, I don't even know his last name."

Well, I could take care of that now. I was sure

53

Claudia was just suffering from low self-esteem. She and Terry had talked for quite a while yesterday (so obviously they could carry on a conversation), and Terry was *still* interested in Claudia, no matter what she thought about herself. I didn't see any reason why Terry and Claud couldn't be friends— or even boyfriend and girlfriend.

"Listen, would you like to phone Claudia?" I asked Terry.

"Of course!" he replied.

"Great. We're all staying at Dawn's house. I'll give you the Schafers' phone number. Claud would love to hear from you."

So I gave the number to Terry. Then I spent the rest of the afternoon with Rosemary, Carter, Alana, and Paul. We must have got pretty caught up in our surfing, because by the time Paul dropped me off at Dawn's, it was after six o'clock.

And Mr Schafer was home.

He didn't look very happy as I climbed over the side of Paul's car and dashed up the front walk.

"Who drove you to the beach today?" he asked me.

I turned around as Paul drove off. Luckily, his tyres didn't squeal.

"Paul . . ." I replied, realizing that I didn't know his last name.

But Dawn had followed her father outside. "Paul Rapkin," she said. "You know. He lives right down the street. His father's Doctor Rapkin. And those other kids are Alana Becker, Rosemary Tanner, and Carter Pape. You know *their* parents, too." Dawn sounded very matter-of-fact.

"Okay," said Mr Schafer. *He* sounded somewhat doubtful, but he let the subject drop, adding, "That reminds me. I'm playing tennis with Carter's father in a couple of weeks."

I let out a sigh of relief.

Everyone else had returned from their outings. Mallory and Jessi (especially Mal) were brimming over with tales of the Max Factor Museum of Beauty. Claud, Kristy, and Dawn had bought matching bracelets at the shopping centre. And Mary Anne had made a long list headed, "Things We *Have* To Do in California".

I looked at Claudia, thinking of my meeting with Terry. I decided not to tell her that I'd given Terry her phone number. I would just wait to see what happened.

Wednesday

Dear Mom and Dad,

Hi! Who are you! I'm having a grate time out here in CAL. We've have allready been to the beach. Yesteday we whent shop — we rode bikes. Dawns house is realy beautiful. Maybe we can put skylites in our roof. That would be so so cool.

Lots of love,
Claudia

Mr. and Mrs. John Kishi

58 Bardford CT

Stoneybrook, Conn. 06800

6th CHAPTER

Claudia

I wrote that postcard on Wednesday. I wrote it *after* everything had happened. (I'll tell you *what* happened in just a minute.) I sort of wanted to write to Mum and Dad about Terry, but I couldn't. I couldn't confide in them about boy stuff. So I stuck to run-of-the-mill things like the beach and the shopping centre. (At least I didn't stoop to discussing the weather, or adding, "Having a wonderful time. Wish you were here ".)

Anyway, what happened was that on Tuesday, after Kristy and Dawn and I got back from the shopping centre (with really great matching charm bracelets), and after everyone had eaten dinner, the phone rang.

"I'll get it!" yelled Jeff. He jumped up from his

game of Nintendo and *raced* for the phone.

"Has he got a girlfriend?" Dawn asked her father.

We all laughed, and Mr Schafer said, "No. Believe it or not, he wants tickets to a Grateful Dead concert. They're going to be playing here next month, and he's dying to go. He's hoping that phone call is Rob saying he's got tickets."

"Jeff's a Deadhead?" said Stacey, giggling.

"Apparently," replied Mr Schafer.

Who were the Grateful Dead? What was a Deadhead? I never did find out because Jeff came back into the living room then, looking disappointed, and saying, "Claudia, it's for you."

For *me*? Who would call me here? The only people I'd given Dawn's number to were my parents.

If they were calling to check up on me, I would kill them.

I picked up the phone in the kitchen. "Hello?" I said. (Thank goodness I didn't say, "Hello, *Mum*".)

"Claudia?" said an unfamiliar voice. (A *boy's* voice.)

"Yes."

"This is Terry. Um, I met you on the beach . . .?" (His voice trailed off in a question, as if he weren't sure I'd remember him.)

"Oh! Oh, hi! Hi," I stammered. And then (drat!) the next words out of my mouth were,

"How did you get this number? How did you know where to find me?"

"Your friend Stacey bumped into me at the beach today. She gave me the number. Anyway, I was wondering. Would you like to go out with me tomorrow? We could have lunch and see a film or something."

I was bowled over. I could barely think. "Well . . . well, yes," I said.

"Great. Just give me your address, and my mum and I will pick you up at midday. Then she'll drop us off at a great shopping centre. It's got a wonderful Italian restaurant, some cinemas and other things. Do you like Italian food?" he asked.

"Yes!" I exclaimed. I still hadn't quite grasped what was happening.

"Terrific. I'll see you tomorrow at midday," he said, when I'd told him where the Schafers live.

"Okay," I replied. "'Bye."

I put down the phone and marched into the living room. "Stacey," I said. "Can I see you for a minute?"

Stacey looked a little wary. "Of course . . ."

"That," I began, "was Terry. The boy—"

"I can't believe he called so soon!" Stacey interrupted. "Wow!"

"Stacey. You had no right to give Terry the Schafers' number. You had no right to interfere in my business." I was furious.

But Stacey's wariness had turned to delight.

61

"Oh, this is great! Are you two going out? We must decide what you're going to wear."

"Stacey—"

"Come on. Where are you going? And when?"

"We're going to an Italian restaurant for lunch tomorrow. And then I think we're going to a film."

"Perfect," said Stacey, who began to paw through the clothes in my suitcase.

"It's not perfect," I countered. "I don't know what to say to him. He's too clever. I don't know anything about—"

"You talked to him for hours yesterday," Stacey pointed out, holding up a wildly patterned sundress.

"Yes, and we ran out of conversation. He said everything that was easy enough for me to understand, and I said everything that I thought would be difficult enough to interest him."

"Oh, *Claud*," said Stacey's response. "Here. Put this on. I want to see you in it."

At five to twelve on Wednesday, I was standing at the Schafers' front door. I was wearing the sundress.

I was a nervous wreck.

Promptly at twelve o'clock, a light grey Toyota pulled up in front of Dawn's house. I wished desperately that somebody—even that rat Stacey —was there to say goodbye to me and to wish me luck. But Stacey was off surfing with those friends of hers again, Mary Anne had just left to sit for Stephie, Jessi was at the TV studio visiting Derek Masters, and Carol had driven Dawn, Kristy, Jeff, and Mal somewhere.

So I composed myself, shouted to Mrs Bruen that my lift was there, and walked sedately to Terry's car. He held open the back door and slid in after me. I didn't really know what to say, but Terry's mother saved the day. She kept asking questions about Connecticut, my family, and my school. At last, she turned the car into the car park of a huge shopping centre. (Not the same one that Dawn and Kristy and I had gone to the day before.) She drove to the back entrance of a restaurant called The Grotto.

"See you at four," she said.

"Okay, Mum. Thanks!" Terry replied.

Four? Four o'clock? I thought. What were we going to do for four hours? (I soon found out.)

Terry led me into the shopping centre so that we could enter the Grotto from the front. We were seated at a table for two and handed menus. Right away, I began to panic. The menu was in Italian! Luckily, before I got too panicky, Terry said, "You know what's really good here? The Fettucini Alfredo."

Fettucini Alfredo. I could deal with that. So I ordered it. Somehow we got through lunch. I don't even remember what we talked about. I'm sure that—whatever it was—it was really boring for Terry. Anyway after lunch, Terry said we might as well make an Italian day of it and go to see this foreign film that was on at one of the cinemas. It was called *Il Tantorino Day Buono Godo*. No, not really. I don't have any idea what it was called. The title was in Italian, and Terry said it so fast I couldn't really catch it.

Okay. So we go into the cinema, sit down, the film starts, and the whole thing is in *Italian*. If you wanted to know what was going on, you had to read the English words that were written across the bottom of the screen. Well, not only couldn't I read fast enough to catch all the words, but the story made no sense to me. It was just a lot of people bicycling around the Italian countryside. Twice, I had to pinch myself so that I wouldn't fall asleep.

After the film, Terry and I walked around the shopping centre, window-shopping until four o'clock. Terry kept talking about the film, but all I could say was, "Yes," and, "I *know*," and, "You're right."

Terry looked impressed. He thought I'd understood the film. That was something, I suppose. At least I hadn't mentioned art or Nancy Drew books or anything like that all day.

When Terry's mum finally dropped me off at Dawn's, I ran inside, hoping to find someone I could talk to—and also planning to kill Stacey.

But the only people there were Mrs Bruen, Jeff, and Carol. My friends were out.

"How was your date?" Carol asked me. She was sitting outside. I joined her.

I tilted my face towards the sun. "It was okay."

"Just okay?"

"I'm not good enough for Terry," I blurted out. "I'm not clever enough. And our interests are so different. What do you think I should do? I feel as if I'm playing a game with him. You know, letting him *think* I'm clever."

"Well," Carol said thoughtfully, "I know people who change to please—"

"What's going on?" interrupted Dawn. She and Kristy stepped through the back door and sat down with Carol and me.

"I was just telling Claudia," said Carol, "that some people try to change their behaviour or their personality in order to make a relationship work—"

"That's stupid!" exclaimed Dawn before Carol could finish.

But I thought it sounded like good advice. Anyway, I was sort of doing that already.

Wednesday

Dear Logan,

Well, you'll never guess what I did today. I babysat! Some of Dawn's friends started a sitting service out here called the We ♥ Kids Club. The We ♥ Kids Club and the BSC had a joint meeting a few days ago, and I got a job with a little girl named Stephie. She's adorable. And we have a lot of things in common. More about Stephie later.

Love
You
Lots, Mary Anne

Logan Bruno

689 Burnt Hill Road

Stoneybrook, Ct. 06800

7th CHAPTER

Mary Anne

Well, Kristy has come up trumps. For once, she's not making me write up a sitting job for our club notebook. Why? I'm not sure. Maybe because the kid I'm sitting for is really a client of the We ♥ Kids Club. Or maybe because she's having too much fun out here to bother with the notebook.

Anyway, I arrived at Stephie's a little before midday. (Mrs Bruen pointed out her house to me.) I'd been wondering why Stephie's father was searching frantically for babysitters when he works full-time, and Stephie's mum died just after Stephie was born. Why didn't he have some sort of permanent arrangement for Stephie?

It turned out that he did. Stephie was being brought up by her father and a nanny. The nanny was sort of like Mrs Bruen. I mean, she didn't live at Stephie's house. But she came over early in the morning and stayed until after dinner five or six days a week. She did some cooking and cleaning while Stephie was at school, but the rest of the time she was like a mum to Stephie. However, it just happened that while Stephie was on her school holiday, her nanny got called away. Some sort of emergency or family problem. So Stephie's dad was booking babysitter after babysitter until the nanny came back.

When I rang the Robertsons' bell that day, a girl who looked about sixteen or eighteen opened the door.

"Hi," she said. "Are you Mary Anne?" (I nodded.) "Oh, good. I'm Lisa Meri, Stephie's morning sitter. Come on in." I entered a house that was similar to Dawn's. It was all on one level and Spanish. The rooms were arranged in a square around a centre courtyard. Almost every room faced into the yard.

"Stephie?" called Lisa. "Mary Anne's here." Lisa Meri turned to me. "Stephie hasn't had her lunch yet. She's feeling a little shy today. I think it's because of all the babysitters. She also said she wasn't hungry, but try to get her to eat something later."

"Okay," I replied.

"Stephie!" Lisa Meri called again. (No answer.)

"As long as she's not coming," I began, "can I ask you a few questions about Stephie's asthma?"

70

"Of course." (I decided I liked Lisa.)

As we walked towards the kitchen, Lisa said, "Do you know what asthma is?"

"Yes," I replied. "It's when you can't breathe because your—bronchial tubes start to close up?"

"Right," said Lisa. "And different things trigger asthma attacks for different people. Sometimes attacks are brought on by too much activity. Some are due to allergies and hay fever. Sometimes they're related to emotions or emotional problems. That's usually when Stephie gets an attack. Lastly, an attack can come on for no reason at all. I mean, you can be *sleeping* and get an attack. What I'm saying, I suppose, is that Stephie can do pretty much whatever she wants. Just be sensitive to her feelings. And remember how shy she is."

"Okay." That shouldn't be a problem. Apart from the asthma, Stephie sounded a lot like me.

Lisa Meri and I were in the kitchen by that time. Lisa showed me Stephie's inhaler and how to use it. She also showed me where her pills were kept. Then, "Stephie!" she called again. "Come out of your bedroom please! Mary Anne's here."

When Stephie still didn't appear, Lisa walked me down a corridor to Stephie's room. I looked inside. It could have been my old bedroom. It looked much too young even for someone Stephie's age. A row of pink bunny rabbits had

71

been stencilled under the ceiling. On her curtains were more pink bunnies. (Also on her lampshade.) The pictures on the walls were of storybook characters—Little Bo Peep and Mother Goose and Peter Rabbit and Babar, the elephant.

Stephie was sitting on her bed with her knees drawn up to her chest. Next to her was a copy of *The Secret Garden*.

"Stephie, this is Mary Anne," said Lisa patiently. "I'm going to leave now, and Mary Anne's going to stay with you until your father comes home."

"Okay," said Stephie in a small voice.

"See you tomorrow!" called Lisa, and as she was leaving, she whispered to me, "Don't worry. Stephie will be fine."

I gave Lisa the thumbs-up sign. Then I slipped into Stephie's room. I wanted to sit with her on her bed, but I didn't want to seem too forward, so I sat in an armchair instead. Stephie didn't even glance at me.

"You know what?" I said. "My room used to look pretty much like yours. My dad decorated it for me."

"Your dad?" repeated Stephie with some interest. "How come your mum didn't help?"

"I haven't got a mum. She died when I was little."

"Same as me," said Stephie.

"You know what else? My dad was really strict

with me. He made up all these rules I had to follow and he even chose my clothes every day."

"*Really?*"

I had Stephie's interest by then, so I sat beside her on the bed. I picked up *The Secret Garden*. "I read this book. I loved it."

"Me, too! I mean, I haven't finished it, but I like it so far."

Stephie turned so that she was facing me, and I looked at her neat brown pigtails and her dark eyes. She could have been me a few years ago.

"Does your father have rules about eating?" asked Stephie.

"He used to," I replied. "Things have changed now, but he most definitely used to."

"Hey, Mary Anne!" (Stephie was really perking up.) "Do you want to go bike riding? You could ride my dad's bike, I bet."

Bike riding? I was afraid of triggering an asthma attack, but all I said was, "Oh, I'm sorry. I can't ride boys' bikes." (This is true.)

"How about roller-skating?"

"I think it's too hot to skate," I said lamely.

Stephie looked disappointed. "Well, could we walk to the park? There are trees in the park," she told me. "We'd be cool."

"I suppose so," I replied. And then I added, "We could take a picnic lunch with us. Lisa said you haven't eaten yet."

"Okay!" Stephie leaped off her bed. And I swear, I thought she was going to have an asthma attack on the spot.

She didn't, of course. She simply grabbed *The Secret Garden* and led me to the kitchen, where we made sandwiches and lemonade. We packed them into a basket along with paper cups and serviettes, and Stephie's inhaler and pills. Then we set off for the park. With each step Stephie took I was sure she was going to start wheezing. But she was fine.

In the park we sat on a grassy spot in the shade of a tree. We ate our sandwiches and drank the lemonade. (I was careful to save some lemonade in case Stephie had an attack and needed to swallow a pill.) When we'd finished eating, Stephie wanted to play on the swings or the slide, but I told her she needed to digest her lunch first. So we talked some more.

"My dad," I said, "used to have a rule that I couldn't use the phone after dinner unless I was talking about homework."

"*My* dad," said Stephie, "will only let me have friends over to play if he knows their parents really, really well."

"Wow!" I replied.

"Mary Anne?" said Stephie. "I like you."

"I like you, too," I told her, smiling. "And now we'd better go home We've got to put our picnic

74

things away. Maybe we could read some of your book."

"Okay!" agreed Stephie.

We spent the rest of the afternoon quietly. When Mr Robertson returned. Stephie greeted him happily, but she seemed subdued. "Daddy? Can Mary Anne babysit for me again?" she asked him. "I really like her."

"Stephie," replied Mr Robertson, "it isn't polite to ask questions like that in front of the person about whom you're speaking."

"All right, Daddy."

"But yes, Mary Anne can come back."

"Oh, thank you!" said Stephie.

"Yes, thank you," I added.

Do you know what? When I returned to Dawn's house I found that Kristy had changed her mind about something. I had to write up my sitting job after all.

Wednesday

Dear Mum and Dad,

    You will not believe the fun we're having here. We have been to the beach and to the Max Factor Museum of Beauty. Today Jessi is going to spend the day watching Derek Masters on the set of <u>P.S. 162</u>. Stacey has been surfing. How are you? How are my darling brothers and sisters?

           See you soon!

           Mallory

Mr. and Mrs. Daniel Pike

134 Slate Street

Stoneybrook, CT 06800

8th CHAPTER

Mallory

Gosh! This morning was really hectic! We all went off in different directions. First, Derek and his father picked up Jessi to take her to the TV studio. Then Stacey left to go surfing. Mary Anne was getting ready to sit for Stephie Robertson, and Claudia was a *wreck*. She was going out to lunch with Terry, and I have never seen anyone so nervous. Jeff went over to Rob's house—and then Carol appeared.

"Oh, boy!" I exclaimed. "I wonder where we'll go today. That beauty museum was great."

Kristy and Dawn were the only ones who didn't have plans so they agreed to come with Carol and me. I could see that Dawn wasn't happy about this, but at least she decided to go.

(Before, she'd said she couldn't even stand being in the same car with Carol.)

"What do you all want to do today?" Carol asked as she bounced into the house. (She's got an awful lot of energy.)

Dawn said immediately. "Stars' homes. Beverly Hills. Hollywood. You can't come to California and not look around for Lucille Ball's house, for example."

"Lucille Ball's house?" shrieked Kristy. "You mean we can see where she used to live?"

"Of course," replied Dawn. "Lots of other famous people, too."

Lucille Ball's house sounded interesting, but there was something I wanted to do a lot more. "Remember that shopping centre we passed on the way to Hollywood yesterday?" I asked everyone. "That really huge one?"

"Yes," said Kristy warily.

"Well, could we go there instead?"

"*Mal*," exclaimed Dawn, exasperated.

"Think of it this way," I said. "Mary Anne will kill us if we go on a star tour without her. She'll *kill* us."

"That's true . . ." agreed Kristy.

"And Washington shopping centre in Connecticut is nothing like the one we passed. This one advertised an ice-skating rink and video hall and *twelve* films and—"

"Okay, okay, okay," said Dawn. "Carol, do

you know how to get to that shopping centre?"

"I think I remember," she replied. "Is that what you really want to do today?"

"Yes!" I cried.

"Yes," said another voice.

We turned around. There was Jeff, looking glum. "Rob and I had a fight," he said pathetically.

"Over what?" asked Carol.

"Over which one of us is the biggest Deadhead."

Carol put her arm around Jeff. She was smiling. "Oh, come on," she said. "You know you'll patch *that* fight up pretty quickly. Let's get going."

So we squeezed into Carol's car and soon we were at . . . the shopping centre.

"Ah," I said. "Just imagine. Skating, eating, buying clothes." (I didn't say anything about buying make-up, but I thought about it.)

"Let's go skating first!" said Kristy as soon as we had parked the car and entered the centre. I was glad she sounded enthusiastic.

So we did. We hired skates and began whizzing around the rink that was on the lowest level of the centre. As I glided along, I looked up.

"Whoa!" I said softly. The centre stretched above us, level after level. It was definitely the biggest I'd ever been in.

When we got tired of skating, we played video

games. Then Dawn wanted to look at shoes, but
Kristy and Jeff said they were starving, so Carol
decided we should eat before we did any
shopping.

"My treat," she added, and led us into a health-
food restaurant. This, of course, made Dawn,
Jeff, and Carol look as though they were in
heaven. Kristy and I had to search around to find
things we could eat, but finally we had all been
served and were eating happily. (Oh, okay. Dawn
didn't look too happy. This was because Carol
was talking a lot, I think, but we ate our meal
without any actual bloodshed.)

And then . . . and *then* . . . Carol paid the bill,
and I cried, "I'm going to the make-up counters!
Meet you at the main entrance in an hour." I
didn't give Kristy or Dawn a chance to say, "But
Mallory, you're not allowed to wear make-up." I
just rushed off. I could hear Carol call, "Okay!"
so I knew the plans were all right.

I had passed the make-up counters on the way
up to the restaurant from the video hall, so I knew
where to go. When I reached the third level, I
gasped.

Surrounding me were lip gloss, eyeliner, mas-
cara, blusher, nail polish, hand and face cream,
powder, and more. An entire floor's worth of
cosmetics.

I was standing at a counter, gazing longingly at

some lipstick, when a saleswoman said, "May I help you?"

To be perfectly honest, I wasn't sure if she could help me or not. I'm definitely not allowed to wear make-up. On the other hand, I was three thousand miles away from my parents. And I wanted to fit in, to be a California girl, to look like some of the girls I'd seen on the beach. If I wore make-up for the next nine or ten days, how would Mum and Dad know?

So I said to the woman, trying to sound very adult, "Yes, thank you. I need a complete make-over."

The woman's eyes lit up. "Come and sit on this stool," she said, motioning over the counter. (I sat.) Then she examined my face with a torch. A *torch*. "Hmm. Not bad," she said slowly. "Not bad at all."

"Can you cover up my freckles?" I asked.

"Oh, certainly."

"Can you dye my hair blonde?"

"What?" The woman looked startled. Then she said, "I suppose so. I mean, *you* could dye your hair . . . How old are you?"

"Eleven," I replied.

"How about trying shampoo-out dye? That way, if your par—I mean, if you don't like it, you could wash it out. Your natural colour would return."

"Great!" I said. I'd been thinking about

shampoo-out dye, anyway. If I used it, I could be a blonde while I was in California, then go back to being a redhead before I got back to Connecticut. (And before my parents saw me.)

"All right. Shall we start with the make-up?" asked the saleswoman.

"Yes." I replied. "Give me whatever I need."

The woman began bustling around behind the counter. Soon a *huge* array of bottles and jars and tubes were spread before me. Also a box. In the box was the shampoo-out hair dye.

"Um, how much is all this going to cost?" I asked the saleswoman.

"Let's see." She added everything up on the till.

When she told me the amount, I couldn't believe it. That was nearly all the spending money I'd brought with me. Oh, well. I decided it was worth it. So I paid the woman.

I had $6.28 left to spend for the rest of my holiday.

That evening, after dinner, all the BSC members gathered in Dawn's room to talk about what we'd done that day. Jessi was in the middle of describing the TV studio she'd been to, when I brought out my bag of make-up.

"*What* is *that*?" asked Jessi, interrupting her own story.

84

"Make-up . . . and hair dye," I added quickly. "It washes out."

"Make-up and *hair dye*?" exploded Jessi.

(My other friends raised their eyebrows or looked at each other.)

"Yes," I said testily. "And now I'm going to dye my hair." Before anyone could say another word, I marched into the bathroom and followed the directions on the packet. When I joined my friends later (quite a bit later), I, Mallory Pike, was a real true (oh, okay, a fake but good-looking) blonde.

"Oh, my lord!" said Claudia, when she and the others saw me.

"Do you like it?" I asked.

"Mallory Pike," said Jessi, who was absolutely simmering, "it's just *not* you. And you've blown all your money on stuff you won't be able to use after our holiday."

"I don't care," I said haughtily. I felt like a real California girl at last.

Saturday

Dear Jessi,

I miss you already and you only left an hour ago. You are so lucky. I want to go to California, too. Squirt is watching a rabbit that is hopping around in our garden. Mama and Daddy are doing boring stuff. Aunt Cecelia is cooking. What are you doing? I love you.

Love,
Becca

Miss Jessica Ramsey
c/o The Schafers
22 Buena Vista

Palo City, Ca. 92800

9th CHAPTER

Jessi

I woke up *really* early on Wednesday. I couldn't wait to see Derek again, and then to go to the TV studio. I've been on plenty of stages in my life, but a TV studio—where a major sitcom is put together every week—was a different story.

I crawled out of my sleeping bag, and started to get dressed. A horrible thought crossed my mind. What if I dressed wrong? How was a person supposed to look in a TV studio? Dressed up? Totally cool? Totally casual? I just didn't know. So finally I put on as cool an outfit as I could find (I had to borrow some things from Claudia's millions of suitcases), and then packed a bag with a casual outfit just in case.

I thought I'd be picked up in a limousine, so I prepared myself for that. I stood in the bathroom, looking in the mirror and pretending to act completely nonchalant—as if I got picked up in a limo every day. I would see the limo, sigh, and say, "How nice. This is just like the one at home." Then I realized I couldn't do that since Derek knew I had no limo at home. Well, at any rate I could get into the limo gracefully and not look too excited. (I hoped.)

I knew that Derek would be coming early in the morning, so I ate breakfast while everyone else was still getting up. When I heard a horn honk, I shrieked, "They're here!"

"I wonder why the chauffeur didn't come to the door for you," said Mal.

I couldn't even answer her. I just ran outside and saw—an estate car driven by Derek's father. Derek and Todd were sitting in the back. I grinned at them.

"Hi, everyone! Hi, Derek! Hi, Todd! Hi, Mr Masters!" In my excitement, I forgot all about the limo and the chauffeur.

"Hi, Jessi!" replied the Masterses.

Both boys were excited. "We're studying insects at my school," Todd told me. "We're going to put on a play. I'm going to be in a dance called 'The Buggie Boogie'. I'm playing an ant."

"And we're doing a really great episode on *P.S. 162* this week," added Derek. "You'll see some special effects."

Mr Masters had stopped the car in front of a nursery, and Todd was climbing out, ready for a day of preschool activities. A teacher met him at the kerb and led him away.

"See you later, Todd!" I called.

Now we were really off to the studio. After a short drive, Mr Masters said, "Well, here we are."

I don't know what I was expecting, but the studio was just a big brick building on a crowded Los Angeles street. It did, though, have a marquee in front (like some cinemas) that said *P.S. 162* in huge letters and numbers.

"Derek, why don't you take Jessi inside while I park the car?" suggested Mr Masters. "You've got the guest pass for Jessi, haven't you?"

"Yup." Derek nodded.

So Derek and I walked into the building together. We had to show our passes everywhere. Well, *I* did. Anybody who saw Derek recognized him immediately. Two people even asked him for his autograph. He took all the attention quite matter-of-factly. Anyway, we reached the fourth floor of the building, and Derek led me through corridors to a door marked Studio 8.

"Here we are!" he exclaimed.

Oh, wow! I thought. I nearly fainted, just imagining what I'd find on the other side of that door.

I have to admit that what I did find was just a

little disappointing—at first. The room was big, dark, full of filming equipment, and crowded with people. But I didn't see a single star from *P.S. 162*, except Derek, of course. Derek showed me to a chair and told me I could sit there and watch everything, but that I'd have to be quiet. He also said his father would join me soon.

The next thing I knew, a man with curly hair said, "Here, Derek. Revised script."

"Okay." Derek turned to me. "Got to go. I have to study this thing."

A short while later, Mr Masters came in. He sat in a chair next to me.

"What's going to happen today?" I asked.

"Well, unfortunately, not a lot of filming, which I know you want to see, but some other interesting things will go on. *And* the whole cast of the show will be here today."

"Really?" I cried. "My sister will be green with envy! Do you think I could get an autograph from the boy who plays Lamont? Becca's got a crush on him."

"Of course," said Mr Masters, smiling.

In a few minutes, the studio began to come to life. The actors entered the set. They were holding scripts and reading from them. The director (I suppose he was the director) kept saying things like, "Derek, try moving over here," or, "Gregg, look at Derek, try moving over here," or, "Gregg, look at Derek when you say that line, okay?"

"What are they doing?" I asked Mr Masters.

"A lot of things," he replied. "They're trying out the scripts, which will probably be changed later today. That's a hard part for Derek. He memorizes his part in one script, then the writers of the show decide the script doesn't work, so they make changes, and Derek has to learn new lines— overnight. Or sometimes in just a few hours.

"They're also blocking the shots. That means they're working out where the actors and actresses look best in each scene— where they should be standing, and how they interact with each other. They may be experimenting with props, too."

I watched Derek—and all the other actors and actresses. I just couldn't believe that I was seeing in person all the stars I watch at home on TV every Friday night. But I was.

Most of the morning was spent rehearsing, occasionally rewriting, and blocking shots. (I felt like a professional, knowing all those things.) Then at eleven-thirty, Derek and the other kids from the show were whisked away.

"Where are they going?" I asked Mr Masters.

"They're being taken off for lessons. While they're filming, they can't go to school, so a tutor works with them for a couple of hours every day."

"Oh," I said, wishing *I* only had to go to school for a couple of hours every day.

While Derek was gone, the first of two really

interesting things happened: special effects. Derek had told me there would be some good ones on this week's show. So I watched, fascinated, as I learned that animation can be done on computers. And that most sound effects are dubbed in. For instance, if an actor walks down a hallway, his shoes might not make enough noise, so the sound-effects people clomp things around to make the footsteps louder.

Mr Masters was telling me some other things when, all at once, the actors and actresses returned to the set—*and* the director made an announcement.

"We need more people for the crowd scene," he said. "We've got a lot of extras, but we need a few more, especially teenagers. If anyone is interested in appearing on *P.S. 162*, come and see me right now."

"Can I go?" I asked Mr Masters. "Please?"

"Of course," he said. "Why not?"

Well, as soon as I stood up, I saw that I wasn't the only one who wanted to be in a crowd scene. An awful lot of other people were hanging around the studio watching, like I was. Brothers, sisters, friends. We rushed to the director. "Whoa!" he said, smiling and holding up his hands. "I only need six more people." He checked us all over carefully. Finally he said, "You, you, you, you, you, and you."

The last "you" was *me*! The director said he

liked my looks. I was terribly flattered—but I had no idea what I'd be in for during the rest of the day. Just getting a simple ten-second shot outside what was supposed to be a high school took over three hours. The director kept calling, "Cut!" and then the cameras would start all over again. I wasn't sure what was wrong each time, but clearly something was. The director looked like a madman, until suddenly he shouted, "Cut! Print! That was excellent!"

My job was over.

I hadn't been paid a cent, but I'd had a great time. And a director had said he liked my looks!

When the filming was over, Derek said to me, "So what did you think?"

"I thought that . . . the day was terrific . . . everyone works harder than I ever imagined . . . and *you* are fantastic as Waldo!"

"Thanks," replied Derek, grinning. Then he added, "You were pretty good in that scene yourself. Honest."

"Yes? I wonder—"

Derek cut me off. "You know, as long as you're out here in California, why don't you try to get on a show or find an agent or something? You know you could do it."

I didn't answer Derek right away. I was thinking over his idea. It sounded like a good one . . .

Thursday

Hi Mum!

Guess what I've been doing.
Surfing! Don't worry. I'm being
careful. I take lessons from an
expert surfer. We've been doing
a lot of other things out here.
Jessi went to a TV studio and now
she wants to be a star. Mary Anne
knows everything there is to know
about California. Oh, I have some
new friends. They're nice. And
the BSC met the We ♥ Kids Club,
another sitting business.

Are you having fun in exciting
Stoneybrook? Ha, ha.

Lots of luv,
Stacey

P.S. Yes, I'm remembering my
insulin and sticking to my diet.

Ms. Maureen McGill

89 Elm Street

Stoneybrook, Ct. 06800

10th CHAPTER

Stacey

Oh, what a day! Nothing ever starts out quietly or easily here, but I suppose that's all right. I like excitement. After all, I was born in New York.

My friends and I have now been in California for about five days. I think Dawn's dad is beginning to feel a little guilty about having to work this week, even though he'll be on holiday next week. At any rate, he asked Carol to come over again in the morning and take us somewhere exciting.

So, of course, Carol turned up. She arrived early, just after Mr Schafer had left for work, and just as Mrs Bruen was organizing breakfast. She came in the van. I suppose she thought we were going to want to go on some big excursion. As it turned out, we needed the van—but not for an excursion.

When Carol arrived, she sat at the breakfast table with us. "Well," she said, "I've got the van. Where are we off to today, you guys?"

(I caught Dawn rolling her eyes. She thought Carol was too old to be saying things like "you guys".)

Mary Anne, tour guide at large, immediately said, "How about Magic Mountain? Or Sea World? Or the California Museum of Science and Industry? Or to the Forest Lawn in Glendale? That was the first of the Forest Lawn cemeteries. The brochure says, 'No trip to the West Coast is complete without a stroll through the park and a visit to the art collections'."

Was Mary Anne out of her mind? A museum of science and industry? Or, worse, a field trip to a *cemetery*?

Luckily, I wasn't the only one who didn't want to go to any of these places. At least not today. Dawn didn't want to go, either. I wanted to go surfing again, and Dawn whispered to me that she couldn't *stand* trooping around an amusement park with Carol. "We can do all those fun things with Dad next week," she said.

"How about a cruise on the *Spirit of Los Angeles*?" suggested Mary Anne.

"NO!" cried Kristy, Dawn, Mal, Claud, Jessi, Jeff, and I.

100

"Okay, okay, okay," said Mary Anne, looking insulted.

"Why don't we just go to the beach again?" said Claud. "I want to work on my tan."

"All right," agreed most of us. But we were still left with a little problem. With two problems, actually. One, if we went to the beach, I wanted to go with my new friends. I did *not* want them to see us getting out of Carol's van. They might think Carol was our babysitter or something. Two, going to the beach still meant that Dawn would have to spend the day with Carol.

Luckily, Jeff solved all our problems. "Hey!" he said. "You know what? I'm sorry, but I don't want to go to the beach with a crowd of girls." (He had the courtesy to add, "No offence.")

"Bring Rob," said Carol.

"No. He still thinks he's a bigger Deadhead than I am. Besides, this is my holiday, too, and there's something I've always wanted to do here."

"What's that?" Dawn asked her brother.

"Go on the NBC Television Studio Tour in Burbank."

"In Burbank?" Carol repeated with a sigh.

"Yes," said Jeff. "It's supposed to be really good. You can get *on camera* in this special little studio. And you see what's happening on whatever shows they're filming that day. And I think there's a trivia game show or something. *Please* can we go there?"

101

"I think everyone else wants to go to the beach," said Carol gently.

"Wait, I've got an idea!" exclaimed Dawn. "Carol, you drop us off at the beach and then take Jeff to Burbank. We're allowed to go to the beach by ourselves, and that way Jeff can go on the tour, too."

Dawn looked extremely proud of herself. She'd just got out of a day with Carol. But Carol didn't know that. She thought the solution was perfect. "Okay with you, Jeff?" she asked.

"I suppose so," he replied.

Meanwhile, *I* was thinking that now I could drive to the beach with my surfing friends. Carol wouldn't care how I got to the beach as long as I got there. She was only going to drop off Claud and Dawn and everyone anyway.

So things were settled. And my friends actually picked me up earlier than they'd said they would—before Carol and the others had left. Why did my friends arrive early? Because Paul wasn't driving, that's why. A different sports car pulled up in front of Dawn's house. It looked as rattly as Paul's, but the doors worked, so that was something. Squashed into the front seat were Paul, Alana, and the driver, a boy I didn't know. In the back seat were Carter, Rosemary, and the surfboards. (Three boards this time.)

"Who's the driver?" asked Dawn, frowning, as

she peered through the front door. She opened the door to see better.

"Don't be so obvious!" I hissed. Then I added, "I don't know. I haven't seen him before. Oh, well. He looks nice. I'll see you all at the beach in a little while, okay?"

"Okay," replied Dawn.

I ran to the car and squeezed myself into the back seat with Rosemary, Carter, and the surfboards.

"Hi, Stacey!" said Alana, turning around. "This is Beau."

"Bo?" I repeated.

"As in B-E-A-U," spelled Beau. "You know, a really romantic guy."

Well, Beau was named all wrong. He should have been named Wild. I'm really glad Carol couldn't see our drive to the beach. Beau would stamp on the accelerator every time we approached an orange light. I almost said, "I thought an orange light meant slow down, not speed through the junction before the light changes to red." But I kept my mouth shut. No one likes a backseat driver.

We took corners that felt as if the car had tipped over onto two wheels. Once, we were in the right-hand lane at a junction and Beau needed to turn left. So he swerved in front of all the cars to our left. One of them almost ran into us, and an oncoming car had to turn sharply to get out of our way. *That* car almost (but didn't) hit a lorry.

Beau, Carter, Alana, Rosemary, and Paul laughed hysterically.

I joined in. This was sort of exciting. No. It was *very* exciting.

By the time we reached the beach I felt as if I could do anything. I felt powerful. I decided not even to take a surfing lesson. I just hired a board and paddled into the water. The first wave that came along looked *huge*. But I rode it in anyway.

I was standing on the shore, shaking the water from my hair, when I heard someone call my name. I turned around to face the water, where Rosemary and everyone were. But they weren't paying attention to anything but the waves.

"Stacey!" the voice called again. "Over here."

It was Claudia. She and the others had just arrived.

I ran to my friends. "Did you see that ride? It was awesome. I'm going out again. Watch me, okay?"

"Okay," agreed the others as they began arranging their things, and Mary Anne set up the parasol.

I paddled out into the water for a second time. And a wave bigger than I'd *ever* seen swelled up behind me. "Oh, boy," I said under my breath.

I stood up on the surfboard and prepared for the ride. The tunnel of water roared over and around me. I could scarcely keep my balance.

And then it happened. Suddenly I wasn't in the wave, I was under it. Water crashed over me, my surfboard was swept out from under my feet, and I felt myself tumbling over and over until finally I came to a halt near the water's edge.

"Stacey! Stacey!" my friends were screaming. "Are you hurt?"

But all I could think was, I hope my swimsuit is still on.

I staggered to the sand and was surrounded by Claud, Dawn, Mal, Mary Anne, Kristy, and Jessi.

"You could have killed yourself!" shouted Dawn. "I'm really worried about you, Stacey. You don't know what you're doing. You're not an expert surfer."

"Oh, I'm fine," I replied. "And I do know what I'm doing. I'm having a great time. Honest."

"Okay," said Dawn. "Just be careful." (I was glad she didn't know about the drive to the beach.)

"See you!" I called, and left to retrieve my surfboard.

                                    Monday
Dear Kristy,
     So how are things in sunny California?
I bet you're having a great time. Things
here are on the boring side. I've played
some ball. Our cousins came over. I worked
on a report for school. (How can teachers
assign reports in the holidays? Doesn't
that sort of defeat the purpose of a
holiday?)   Have fun! If you see any
cute girls, tell them Bart Taylor said
hello. (Just kidding.)
                              Love ya,
                               Bart

Kristy Thomas
c/o the Schafers
22 Buena Vista

Palo City, Ca. 92800

11th CHAPTER

Kristy

Hmm. I may have forgotten to mention that I have a sort of boyfriend. His name's Bart, and he coaches a team of little kids who like to play softball. The team is Bart's Bashers. *I* coach a team called Kristy's Krushers. Our teams are rivals and Bart and I used to be rivals, too. But now we're, well . . . we're very, very good friends. Sometimes I think he's my boyfriend, but I'm not sure. Anyway, it was nice to hear from him.

I was sorry that Bart wasn't having such a good holiday, especially when I was. I'd been to the beach, to some shopping centres, and I'd had plenty of time to hang around with my friends. Even when we were just chatting, we were having fun. However, this was before the members of the We ♥ Kids Club spent the night at Dawn's house on Thursday. That evening wasn't exactly the high point of the holiday for me.

At about six o'clock, Sunny, Jill, and Maggie turned up at Dawn's house with their sleeping bags. All nine of us were going to sleep on the floor in the games room. We were wall-to-wall girls.

"Disgusting," said Jeff. "I'm sleeping at Rob's."

"I thought you two had fallen out," said Dawn.

"We had. But our fight's over."

"Oh, yes? Who's the bigger Deadhead?" I asked.

"Neither one of us. We decided that Rob's brother is. Anyway, I know lots more about hockey than they do. If I still lived on the East Coast, I'd be the biggest Islanders fan in the world."

With that, Jeff left.

The members of the BSC and the We ♥ Kids Club looked at each other. Then we all began to laugh.

"What are we going to eat?" Sunny asked Dawn.

Oh, no, I thought. Probably aubergine and celery pizza.

But Dawn said, "Whatever we want." So we raided the fridge and I actually had a peanut butter-and-honey sandwich. We took our food to the games room and ate on our laps on the floor.

I had eaten exactly one bite of my sandwich when Dawn blurted out, "I can't *stand* Carol! She's such a busybody. And she thinks she's one of us. Or anyway, she acts as if she's one of us."

"But Dawn," said Jessi, "she's just trying to make sure we have fun while your father's working. She's been a chauffeur and a tour guide—"

"And she let Mallory dye her hair blonde," said Dawn sarcastically.

"She didn't *let* me. She didn't know what I was going to do," said Mal.

"Well, she should have."

Mal sighed. There was no arguing with Dawn when it came to Carol.

"*I'm* having a great time," said Stacey enthusiastically. "California's great."

"Oh, yes?" said Sunny.

"Yes. I've learned how to surf. I had a couple of lessons and now I can ride the waves." Stacey made "ride the waves" sound like floating through the sky on cottonwool clouds.

"You've learned how to surf after just a couple of lessons?" asked Maggie incredulously. "Gosh. It took me ages."

"I've found new friends here, too," Stacey went on. "They're great. We drive to the beach almost every day."

"I went to a TV studio and watched them filming *P.S. 162.* I know Derek—you know, the boy who plays Waldo—personally," said Jessi.

111

"You *do*?" squeaked Jill. "I mean, he's much too young for me, of course, but I don't know any real TV stars."

"Derek's a nice kid," said Jessi. "I watched the filming and rehearsing all day, and Derek's a pro . . . Oh, and guess what I did late in the afternoon?" (Jessi didn't give anyone a chance to guess.) "I was in a *crowd scene*. I'm going to be on one of the episodes that's coming up!"

"You're kidding!" cried Sunny.

"No." Jessi looked pleased with herself. "*And* Derek said I should try to get into a film or something out here. The director of *P.S. 162* said he likes my looks. Can you believe it? Perhaps I'll get an agent."

"Gosh!" said Mary Anne, even though she'd heard the story about a hundred times.

There was a moment of silence. Then Stacey said, "Claud found a boyfriend."

"I did not!" cried Claud.

"Well, what do you call Terry?" asked Dawn.

"I call him . . . for dinner!" joked Claud.

"Seriously. You and Terry had gone out—"

"And that's another thing," interrupted Dawn loudly. "I don't think you should change your personality just for Terry."

"But Carol said that—"

At that moment, Carol, who was spending the evening at Dawn's, stuck her head into the games room. "Everything all right in here?" she asked.

"Just fine," said Dawn.

"Okay." Carol left.

"Dawn! She probably heard us talking about her," exclaimed Mary Anne.

"I don't care," replied Dawn sulkily. She threw down her fork. "Carol makes me lose my appetite. She should act her age—and clear off."

Maggie changed the subject, although it wasn't a subject I wanted to hear about. "Hey, Kristy, she said. "Don't forget that you're sitting for Erick and Ryan on Saturday."

I was insulted. "How could I forget a thing like that?" I asked.

"Uh-oh," said Dawn. "I've just thought of something."

"Not Carol again," said Mallory, who was examining her hair in a hand mirror.

"*No*. Not Carol again," replied Dawn testily. "Dad told me last night that he's taking us all to the Universal Studios tour on Saturday."

"Awesome!" shrieked Jessi. "That's great!"

"Oh, my lord! I've been dying to go there," cried Claud.

"Yes. You'll see all these wonderful sets from real films and TV shows," added Stacey.

"And you learn how special effects are done," said Mary Anne. "And you'll experience an earthquake and a collapsing bridge. And Woody Woodpecker walks around . . ." Our talking guide book must *really* have read up on Universal Studios.

"So what's the problem?" asked Mal.

"Kristy's babysitting on Saturday, that's what," replied Dawn.

"Then I'll bring Erick and Ryan with us," I said. "That's no problem—as long as your dad and their parents agree. It'll be a nice outing for them."

"Whoa, whoa, whoa!" said Sunny, holding up her hands. "Are you crazy? Take *Erick* and *Ryan* to a place as big as Universal Studios? You have no idea what you'll be in for. They'll be all over the place. They'll—"

"*I*," I interrupted Sunny, "can handle children, thank you. I'm chairman of the *first* babysitting club. I *know* what I'm doing."

"But you *don't* know Erick and Ryan."

"Doesn't matter," I muttered.

"Gosh," said Mary Anne wistfully, "if we do make an outing of Saturday, it's too bad Stephie couldn't come with us. She and I have so much in common."

"Why can't she come?" asked Jill.

"Because of her asthma," said Mary Anne matter-of-factly.

"Oh, *that* doesn't matter," said Maggie. She must have seen the horrified look on my face because she added, "Stephie can be active. She really can. She has to be a little careful, of course, but she'd have her inhaler and her pills with her. She always does. I think she'd *love* to go with you."

So who was Maggie anyway? The Queen of Babysitters?

"I don't know—" I started to say.

But Mary Anne interrupted. "I'm going to phone Stephie's father tomorrow," she said. "I mean, if it's all right with you lot, and with your father, Dawn."

"Fine with me," answered Dawn.

"And *I'm* going to phone Erick and Ryan's parents," I said. "The boys would probably love all that earthquake stuff."

Sunny, Maggie, and Jill looked at each other. Their look plainly said, "Kristy doesn't know what she's doing."

So what? I thought. *They're* the irresponsible members of the club with the stupidest name I've ever heard of.

Luckily—I mean, before a fight broke out—Mary Anne said, "What else will we do next week, Dawn? Go to Magic Mountain? Knott's Berry Farm? The Los Angeles Zoo? Tour star's homes?"

"Anything we want," replied Dawn. And then she added, "Miss Tour Guide," and threw a pillow at Mary Anne, which started a brill pillow fight.

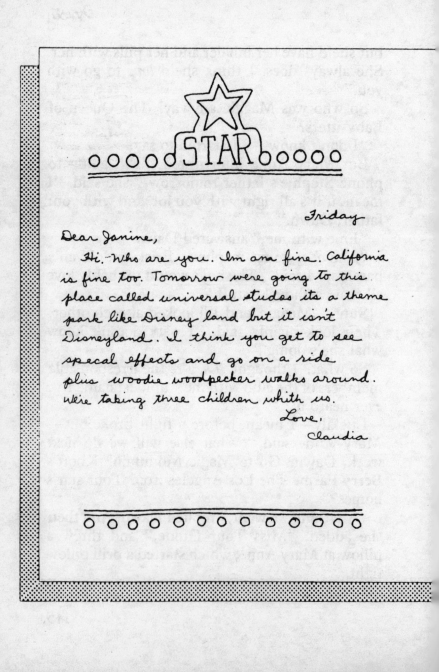

STAR

ooooo STAR ooooo

Friday

Dear Janine,
    Hi. Who are you. Im ana fine. California
is fine too. Tomorrow were going to this
place called universal studes its a theme
park like Disney land but it isn't
Disneyland. I think you get to see
specal effects and go on a ride
plus woodie woodpecker walks around.
We're taking three children whith us.
                    Love,
                        Claudia

○ ○ ○ ○ ○ ○ ○ ○ ○ ○ ○ ○ ○ ○

Janine Kishi

58 Bradford

Stoneybrook, Connec 06800

12th CHAPTER

Claudia

I was getting awfully good at not telling my family what was *really* going on out in California. I mean, we *were* going to Universal Studios on Saturday, and Erick, Ryan, and Stephie had all been given permission to go with us, but the important thing that was happening to me was that I had another date with Terry.

This time, I'd been given *plenty* of advice by my friends about how to handle the date. And I tried to take it. After all, I wanted Terry to like me.

"Just be yourself," said Dawn on Friday morning.

"And don't worry so much about what *you* think Terry thinks of you," added Stacey, who was already wearing her swimsuit.

119

"But he talks about all these things like world affairs . . . and French," I said. "How am I supposed to answer him? Say, 'Hmm. Sounds like a Nancy Drew book I read once.'"

Mallory giggled. "Don't say anything, then," she advised. "Maybe he'll think you understand him. After that, change the subject."

"I go back to what I said before. *Be yourself*," said Dawn emphatically.

"Honestly," added Jessi. "No matter what you think, you're not *inferior* to Terry. You're just very different from him. I'm sure you two can have a good time together. A *very* good time. Think positive."

"Positively," corrected Mary Anne.

"Whatever," said Jessi.

Terry and his mum were calling for me late on Friday afternoon.

"Is a French restaurant all right with you?" Terry asked as we stopped at a junction and waited for the lights to change.

"Oh, yes." I checked my outfit, wondering how fancy the restaurant was. I decided I looked fine. For one thing, despite what Dawn had said about "being myself", I hadn't dressed like myself at all. Ordinarily I would have worn some wild combination of trousers and high-topped trainers and large jewellery. But for this evening I had borrowed a very tame dress from Dawn. I think it might have been a Laura Ashley dress. It was simple—a small-flowered print with short sleeves, a proper waistline, and a nice lace collar. Then I had borrowed a pair of flat pink shoes from Mary Anne.

I looked like a nine-year-old. Or maybe a grandmother.

Terry's mum soon pulled into a car park and said, "Okay. Here you are. I'll be back for you at seven-thirty."

"Okay. Thanks, Mum!" said Terry. He climbed out of the car and held the door open for me.

"Yes, thanks," I added as Terry closed the door.

As soon as we were inside the restaurant, I was glad I was dressed the way I was. My outfit looked as tame as the others I saw. And Terry, who was wearing a suit, just blended in with the rest of the boys. The only difference between us and everyone else in the restaurant was that we were about thirty years younger than they were.

Terry stepped up to a man wearing a dinner jacket standing behind a little desk. "Reservation for Laing for two, six o'clock," Terry said expertly.

"Ah," replied the man. "*Mademoiselle? Monsieur?* Right this way, *s'il vous plaît.*"

(*S'il vous plaît?* I had a feeling I was in for a rough evening.)

The man wearing the dinner jacket led us to a

121

small table by a window overlooking a little pond. I hadn't been sure of the meaning of the word *intimate* until then—but suddenly it hit home. *Intimate* is a small table for two, set so that the diners sit *next* to each other, not opposite each other. It's a table covered with a pink cloth, and it's a vase with a single rose in it. It's a candle burning in a low glass holder that sends patterns of light across the table. And it's sitting so that your hand is about a quarter of an inch away from the hand of the boy you're with. Your hands aren't touching, but they feel as if they are. Terry and I had been sitting and just sort of looking out at the duck pond (I noticed that neither of us moved our hands), when a waiter appeared at our table and handed menus to Terry and me.

"*Voilà,*" he said. "*Les menus. Aujourd'hui les spécialités de la maison sont . . .*" (Whoa! I was in *big* trouble.)

As soon as the waiter left, Terry said, "Well, that chicken special sounds good. I think I'll have that."

Oh. So those were the specials.

I picked up my menu. "The chicken does sound good," I agreed, "but I want to see what's on the menu."

"Do you want any help?" Terry asked me.

Did I want help? No. I mean, I *can* read, after all.

122

I opened the menu. *The entire thing was in French.*

Oh, my lord! I thought.

But I kept my composure. I'm not a picky eater. There aren't too many things I won't at least try to eat. So I picked out something on the menu that looked easy to pronounce. It was just one word. *Escargots.*

When the waiter returned to the table, he said, "*Êtes-vous prêtes?*"

"Yes, we're ready." (At least Terry was speaking in English. That meant I could, too.) "I'll have the chicken special," he said.

"*Trés bien,*" replied the waiter. "*Et vous, mademoiselle?*"

I opened the menu, pointed to my choice, and said "And I'll have the—"

"Ah. *Escargots. Bien.*" The waiter left.

I glanced at Terry and found him looking at me—wide-eyed. "You like *escargots?*" he said. (I noticed that neither he nor the waiter had pronounced the "t" or the "s" at the end of the word, and I was glad I hadn't tried to pronounce it.)

"Oh, yes. We often have . . . have *escargots* at home."

"Wow!" said Terry.

"So," I said, as another waiter placed glasses of water in front of us, "what do you think about the situation in, um, the Soviet Union?"

"Glasnost?" was Terry's reply.

Glasnost? What was that? "Uh, yes. Glasnost," I said.

"Well, I'm not sure yet. I think the countries that are gaining their independence are going to be in for a tough time, don't you?"

"Oh, definitely," I replied. Terry waited for me to go on, but of course I had nothing to say. Luckily, I was saved by Terry.

"Personally I'm worried about the greenhouse effect."

Terry was worried about problems with greenhouses? What could be wrong with greenhouses? Maybe I didn't have as much to be upset about as I thought.

Wrong.

Dinner arrived. And guess what the waiter put down in front of me? A whole plate of *snails*. I'm not kidding. You know those slugs that slime around in gardens? Well, that was what was on the plate, except that they were in shells and smothered by some kind of sauce.

I almost said, "Excuse me, but there's been a mistake. I don't know how it happened, but you've got a snail problem in your kitchen."

However, both Terry and the waiter just smiled at me. Then the waiter said, "*Bon appétit,*" and left.

Let me tell you, swallowing those snails was *not* easy. I felt as if I was swallowing garlic-coated rubber. And I kept thinking of that song that goes, "*Nobody likes me, everybody hates me, guess I'll go eat worms. First one was slimy, second one was grimy, third and fourth came up.*" There's more to the song, but as soon as I thought of the worms coming up, my snails almost came up. I coughed. Then I drank a lot of water.

"Are you okay?" asked Terry.

"Oh, fine," I said, still choking.

I tried to think of some subject that would interest him. I didn't tell him about my art or the BSC or Mimi. But I remembered the name of an adult book Janine had read recently and asked him if he'd read it. He hadn't.

By the end of the meal, I was pretty sure I'd made a complete fool of myself. I was also pretty sure I wouldn't see or hear from Terry again.

I cried in the car on the way home, but Terry didn't notice.

Tuesday

Dear Mallory,

Hi! How is California? Is it really sunny and warm with palm trees and convertible cars like on T.V, or is that just its ~~repp~~ ~~repa~~ ~~repla~~ reputation? (Mom had to help me spell that.)

I'm writing lots of poetry. Here's a springtime poem. I hope you like it.

Hello, baby birdie, with your funny yellow belly. And your light blue eyes and your tiny, tiny feet.

Have you seen the flowers or the children outside playing, or the bright green grass or felt Mr. Sun's new heat? Spring is here!

Lots of Love,
Vanessa

Mallory Pike
c/o The Schafers
22 Buena Vista

Palo City, Ca 92800

13th CHAPTER

Mallory

I liked hearing from my sister. I especially liked her poem.

I'm sure she'll be a poet when she grows up.

But I have to admit that I was more excited about the fact that it was Saturday. Mr Schafer was officially on holiday—and we were going to Universal Studios! The day was all planned. Jeff was coming with us, but Carol wasn't. (Dawn couldn't have been happier.) However, we were borrowing Carol's friend's van again. We had to. *Twelve* people were making the trip to Hollywood: the seven members of the BSC, Jeff, Mr Schafer, Erick, Ryan and Stephie. (I think Carol didn't go because she couldn't *fit*. Or maybe she was just sick of all of us.)

Thanks to Mary Anne, I'd read up on Universal

Studios the day before, and guess what I'd found out? The tour guides pick people from the audience to demonstrate special effects and things. Okay. So now I looked *really* great, like a real California girl, and here was my chance to get chosen to stand up in front of a lot of people and show them exactly how good I looked.

On Friday night I re-dyed my hair. The woman at the beauty counter had said it was a shampoo-out dye, and I'd washed my hair several times since I'd dyed it. It didn't look much less blonde to me than before, but I wanted to be on the safe side at Universal Studios.

Then, on Saturday morning, I woke up extra early. I spent a whole hour putting on my make-up. In fact, I stayed in the bathroom so long I was forced to *stop* putting on make-up when Jessi pounded on the door and said, "What are you *do*ing in there?"

"Putting on my make-up," I replied. I closed one eye and smeared eyeliner along it. It looked rather thick, but I guessed that was okay.

"Well, hurry up. Everyone else needs to get in the bathroom, too. And some of us need to get in there badly."

"Okay. Just let me do this other eye."

"Mallory!"

"They have to match!" I cried.

Unfortunately, it took a while to make the two eyes match. By the time I got out of the bathroom,

no one looked very pleased with me. And
certainly, no one said I looked nice or anything.
Oh, well. They'd change their minds when I was
selected for a special demonstration.

After breakfast, we piled into the van. We
stopped at Stephie's house first, and picked her
up.

"Have you got your inhaler?" Mary Anne
asked her nervously. "And your pills?"

"Yes," replied Stephie. She sounded shy and
sat as close to Mary Anne as possible without
actually climbing in her lap.

Then we picked up Erick and Ryan. They were
quite different from Stephie! They jumped into
the van, both wearing sun-visors, and immediately
announced who they were.

"Hi! I'm Erick, and I'm eight!"

"I'm Ryan, and I'm six!"

"I," said Kristy, "am your babysitter. My
name is Kristy Thomas, and I'm thirteen. Okay.
Strap yourselves in next to me, and we'll be ready
to go."

"I can't strap myself in," said Ryan. "My
sword's in the way."

"What sword?" asked Kristy. (Ryan was
empty-handed.)

"My super-power sword. Whoosh, whoosh,
whoosh."

Do you get the picture? That's pretty much the
way the drive to Hollywood went. Erick and Ryan

(who had to be separated, Kristy sitting between them) made sound effects and played loud imaginary games during the entire trip. Stephie snuggled up to Mary Anne—and cried once when Erick said he was going to zap her.

We were all starting to wonder if today's outing was such a good idea, especially when Mr Schafer began scowling at us in the rear-view mirror. And I, for one, wasn't happy sitting squashed between Jessi and Stacey. My hair was getting rumpled and I was sweating. I hoped my make-up wasn't running.

Anyway, we finally saw a huge sign that said Universal Studios.

"There it is! There it is!" shrieked Erick.

Jeff rolled his eyes.

We saw a few more signs and followed them up a hill and into a HUGE car park. An attendant showed us where to park the van, and then we all tumbled out.

"Is my hair okay?" I asked Jessi.

"It's *fine*," she snapped.

Gosh! What was wrong with her?

We began walking towards the entrance to Universal Studios.

"Is this anything like Derek's TV studio?" Claud asked Jessi.

"Not so far," replied Jessi, looking awed.

Universal Studios is more like a theme park—such as Disneyland—except that TV shows and

131

films are actually filmed there. First we passed a
big cinema where about a hundred films were
being shown. Jeff wanted to see one, but luckily,
no one else did. So we went into the park. There
was just one problem. I had spent almost all my
money on make-up and hair dye. I didn't have
nearly enough to buy a ticket into the park.

"Jessi?" I whispered. (I didn't want Mr
Schafer to know what bad shape I was in,
money-wise.)

"Yes?"

"Can I borrow some money?"

Jessi made a face, but she lent me the money.

"I'll keep track of what I borrow," I said.
"Promise. I'll pay you back when we get to
Stoneybrook."

"You mean you're going to need more money?"
asked Jessi.

"Well, I've only got six dollars and twenty-
eight cents left," I replied. "And we're going to
be out here for another week."

Jessi sighed heavily.

Anyway, we all paid for our tickets, went into
the park, and saw . . . Woody Woodpecker! It was
just like a Disneyland or Disney World, where
Mickey and Minnie and Goofy and Donald walk
around. To no one's surprise, Erick and Ryan
wanted their picture taken with Woody. And that
was when we realized something. Not one of us
had thought to bring a camera.

132

"Hey," said Jeff, "I bet we can buy some disposable cameras at one of the gift shops."

So we did just that. Mr Schafer, Jeff, Dawn, Kristy, Claudia, Jessi, Stacey, Mary Anne, and Erick all bought cameras. They were pretty cheap and I wanted one, too, but I decided I'd better borrow money for only the most important things.

After picture taking with Woody Woodpecker, we got into a queue for the tram tour through the studios. The next tour was going to start in fifteen minutes, and we didn't want to miss it. So we filed through the turnstiles and followed a crowd of other people along a winding pathway up a hill. We hadn't walked far, though, when Claudia clutched my arm and whispered, "Oh, my lord!"

"What? What is it?" I asked.

"Look at that tree. *Frankenstein's* leaning against it."

The Frankenstein looked real enough, but he was standing still as stone. "He's fake," I said. "He's just a prop. They're trying to amuse us while we wait for the tour to begin. See? He— Aaargh!" The "fake" Frankenstein had thrust his hand out and patted my hair. But by the time I looked back at him, he was a statue again.

I noticed Mary Anne clutching Stephie protectively, but Stephie didn't seem at all concerned, not even when Frankenstein reached towards her.

133

Neither did Erick nor Ryan. They were laughing hysterically.

The queue continued to move, and soon attendants were seating us on trams. The trams consisted of rows of six seats. (We took up two entire rows!) Then an announcer at the front of the tram introduced himself and said that we would be going to the special-effects stage first. We would watch a film, and then volunteers would be chosen to help demonstrate the effects. Ah! Just what I'd been waiting for. Who could resist a beautifully made-up blonde!

Apparently our tour guide could. The first two volunteers had to be a lot older than any of us BSC members, had to weigh more than most of us did, had to be a certain height, and had to be wearing shorts or trousers. The only requirement I met was the trousers. The next volunteer had to have a good sense of humour and extremely short hair. The fourth volunteer had to be between the ages of five and ten. I couldn't believe it.

"I look *great*," I said to Jessi, "but I can't be a volunteer."

"Rotten luck," she replied.

But she perked up when we sat down in the stage area and saw how special effects are achieved. We saw how Elliott, the little boy in *E.T.*, flew through the air on his bicycle. ("I knew that," said Jessi.) We saw how Fred Astaire tap-danced on the ceiling. ("Knew that, too," said Jessi. "I learned all this on the set of *P.S. 162*.")

We learned how sound effects are made, how an amusement park was flattened in a film called *1941*, and how Los Angeles appeared to be flattened in *Earthquake*.

I was fascinated, but I would have been even more interested if Jessi hadn't been acting like such a know-all. I almost told her to shut up, but I realized that I needed to borrow money from her. Besides, we're best friends and we'd never had a fight.

I didn't want to start one then.

Saturday

Dear Karen and Andrew,

So what are you ~~two~~ up to? Today we went to a place called Universal Studios. A lot of films and TV shows are made there. We saw the shark from Jaws and lots of other **great** things. Say hi to Emily and Nannie and everyone else.

Love you!
Kristy

Karen and Andrew Brewer

1210 McLelland Road

Stoneybrook, Ct. 06800

14th CHAPTER

Kristy

Okay, so maybe Erick and Ryan are a little on the active side, but they don't seem like the wild monsters that the girls in the We ♥ Kids Club had described. The way those girls talked, you'd have thought Erick and Ryan needed dog leads. But no. They were just excited. After they realized Frankenstein was real, Erick took pictures of him. However, they did become just a tiny bit wild by the time we were ready to board the tram, so I put them in the centre two of the six seats. Then I sat next to Erick, and Stacey sat next to Ryan. That seemed like a good arrangement. Sitting in the middle of the tram, the boys couldn't lean over the side or stick their arms out, things the tour guide specifically told *every*body not to do. They couldn't be anything but well behaved.

However, when the tram stopped for the special-effects stage, the tour guide said, "Before we move inside, we'll watch a short film and choose volunteers for later on. This is your *last chance* to use the toilets on the tour. They're right over there" (he pointed) "and you can easily catch up with the tour while we're watching the film."

Erick and Ryan immediately said (almost in one voice), "I've got to go to the toilet." Erick added, "And we can go by ourselves. We're allowed."

"Okay," I replied, thinking that I could really show up Sunny, Jill, and Maggie. I'd prove to them that the boys could be responsible. "I'll wait outside for you," I told them.

I positioned myself by the entrance to the gents', feeling a little embarrassed. "We'll catch up with all of you in a few minutes," I called to my friends.

"Okay," Mary Anne replied.

The boys ran into the toilets and I stood outside and waited. And waited . . . and waited . . . and waited.

Finally I saw Stacey beckoning to me from the entrance to the building where the film was being shown.

"What?" I yelled. "I can't leave here."

Stacey ran to me. "The film's over," she

announced. "They're choosing the volunteers and then we'll be going to the stage. Hurry up. What are the boys doing?"

I shook my head, and an uncomfortable thought flitted through my brain, but I didn't have time to pay attention to it. "Get Jeff," I said urgently. "He can go in the gents' and see what's happening."

I started to peep inside myself, but before I could see a thing, I felt too embarrassed and ducked back out. Thankfully, Jeff was running towards me.

"Jeff, go inside and get Erick and Ryan. Quick!"

"Okay." Jeff disappeared into the gents'. A few heart-pounding moments later, he returned with the boys. They were dripping wet.

"What was going on in there?" I asked.

"These two," said Jeff, who was holding each boy by an arm, "were squirting each other with water and throwing wet paper towels at the ceiling."

"Three of them got stuck up there!" said Ryan proudly.

"But you haven't got time to fool around like that," I said. "We've got to keep up with the tour. Otherwise we'll get lost."

"Yes," said Jeff. "Besides, I don't think you'll want to miss what's about to happen next."

"What?" asked Erick excitedly.

140

"They need a volunteer to play Elliott in that scene from *E.T.* where he rides E.T. through the air in his bike basket."

"Awesome!" exclaimed Erick.

"Cool!" said Ryan.

The boys and I ran to catch up with the tour and got there just in time to hear our guide say, "This volunteer needs to be between the ages of five and ten."

A field of hands began to wave wildly, among them Erick's, Ryan's and Jeff's.

'Okay," said our guide. "how about you?" He pointed to . . . Jeff!

"All right!" Jeff exclaimed, and was led off by an assistant who promised Mr Schafer that Jeff would be returned to him after he had demonstrated the effect.

I was grinning like crazy for Jeff (who was grinning like crazy, too), until I realized something. Erick and Ryan were whining—loudly.

"Not fair!" shouted Ryan.

"*I* wanted to be Elliott," cried Erick.

"You two," I whispered, "keep the noise down. You're making a scene."

"But it *wasn't fair*!" Ryan was shrieking.

People were beginning to stare at us, so as we filed into the seats of the first special-effects stage, I put an arm around each boy and covered their mouths with my hands.

Ryan tried to bite me!

141

"Cut . . . it . . . out . . . and . . . behave," I said between clenched teeth.

The boys didn't say a word (which was better than yelling), and they appeared to be bored during the entire special-effects show. They even booed when Jeff rode Elliott's bicycle.

However, when the special effects were over and we boarded the tram again, the rest of the tour was just one big ride. The boys were in seventh heaven, although they did their share of complaining.

"We can't see! Why're we stuck in the middle?" they said loudly. They leaned across Stacey and me. (I tried not to think of the warnings that had been given to me by the members of the We ♥ Kids Club.)

Even though they complained, the boys loved everything. They loved seeing the house from the old show *Leave It to Beaver*. They loved seeing how a building could *look* as though it was on fire. They loved seeing the town square from the film *Back to the Future*. They loved seeing the sets for current TV shows, and they loved the fact that most of the buildings were false fronts. Nothing was behind them. They just made a street look authentic for a shot of a town.

But as far as Erick and Ryan were concerned, the best parts of the tour were the ones that were like amusement park rides.

We rode over a bridge and our guide suddenly

cried out, "Uh-oh! this doesn't look safe to me . . . Oh, no! I think the bridge is col—"

"It's collapsing!" Ryan finished for him as the middle section of the bridge seemed to drop out from under us.

My heart nearly stopped beating, but Erick stood up and yelled, "Cool!"

Instantly, the guide stopped his talk and said loudly, "Please! Sit down! The bridge is only fake, but I don't want anyone hurt. You are to stay in your seats and keep your arms *inside* the tram."

"They weren't out," said Erick rudely.

"Then just sit down, please." The guide sounded annoyed, and I couldn't blame him. I was annoyed myself.

After that, things on the tour became a little scarier. A gigantic King Kong loomed at us out of the darkness of a tunnel, baring teeth and fangs. Bruce, the shark in *Jaws*, reared up from what looked like a lake, also baring sharp teeth. A flash flood poured down on us. The boys screamed, took photos, and continued to jump out of their seats. I bet our tour guide wanted to throw Erick, Ryan, and probably me right off the tram.

But at that point, something interesting happened. We entered another dark tunnel and our guide (eyeing Erick and Ryan) said, "Uh-oh! I think I feel the ground shaking. Whoa!—We're

143

in for another earthquake. And it's an eight point three on the Richter scale."

"An earthquake?" whispered Ryan trembling.

"But we've just had one," added Erick in a hushed voice.

Suddenly things were happening everywhere. A fire and flood began. Debris fell from above us. We were surrounded by noise. Finally a massive train crash occurred—and Stacey and I found ourselves with a terrified little boy in each of our laps.

"It's only fake," we whispered soothingly, as the doors at the end of the tunnel opened and we emerged into safety and sunlight.

From then on, the boys stayed in our laps. I told them that they had to because they couldn't be trusted to sit on their own. What I had discovered was this: Maggie, Sunny and Jill had been right. The boys were wild. They did need to be controlled. Maybe I wasn't the only one who knew a lot about kids. Maybe I wasn't the only babysitting expert.

And I'd learned something else that day. Ryan and Erick had fears, too. However, I could allow them to hide their fears and appear to be the tough little boys they wanted to be by telling them they *had* to behave, and laying down a few rules. Then they looked as if they were responding to my orders, instead of acting scared.

144

I was letting them save face—keep their image—and control them at the same time.

I was pretty proud of myself.

TUESDAY

DEAR MARYANNE,

BY THE TIME YOU GET THIS POSTCARD,
IT'LL PROBABLY BE SATURDAY. I HOPE
YOU'RE DOING SOMETHING REALLY FUN.
ARE YOU GOING TO DISNEYLAND? IT'S
PRETTY BORING HERE. HUNTER'S
ALLERGIES ARE BOTHERING HIM AND
MUM HAD TO TAKE HIM TO THE DOCTOR.
I BABYSAT FOR JENNY PREZZIOSO
TODAY. ALL SHE CAN TALK ABOUT IS
THE NEW BROTHER OR SISTER SHE'S
GOING TO GET. (SHE WANTS TO
NAME IT YUCKY TOILET.)

LOTS OF LOVE,
LOGAN.

MARY ANNE SPIER % THE SCHAFERS

22 BUENA VISTA

PALO CITY, CA 92800

15th CHAPTER

Mary Anne

From the moment Stephie got in the van with us I began to wonder whether I'd done the right thing by asking her along on our outing. The members of the We ♥ Kids Club had said it would be good for her, and so had Lisa Meri. And of course Stephie's father had said it was all right for her to go. He should know best.

But in the van on the way to Hollywood, Stephie was so clingy—and so different from Erick and Ryan. Was she going to have an emotional asthma attack? Was she frightened being with so many strangers, and on her way to an equally strange place? I kept one arm around Stephie during the entire ride, and the other hand on her inhaler, which she had given me and was in my pocket. I was really relieved when we parked

the van and Stephie was still sitting next to me,
breathing normally.

We ambled towards the theme park. Stephie
held my hand and didn't say a single word. But I
could see her looking around with interest. She
was taking everything in, in her own quiet way.

And then—we entered the world of Universal
Studios and Stephie came to life. Her eyes
positively lit up.

"Look, Mary Anne!" she cried. "There's
Woody Woodpecker! . . . Ooh, and look at this
shop. Look at all the stuff in it. Can I buy a
T-shirt? And this hat? And this stuffed animal?
P*lease*? Daddy gave me spending money."

"Why don't we wait until we're leaving before
we buy souvenirs? Otherwise, we're just going to
have to lug them around all day."

"Okay," said Stephie affably, jumping from
one foot to the other.

I almost said, "Calm down," but thought
better of it.

Soon we were in the queue for the tram
ride through the studios. I spotted a fake
Frankenstein leaning against a tree and pointed
him out to Stephie, so that she would be prepared
when we walked by him. To my horror, the
"fake" Frankenstein jumped out and tugged at
Stephie's pigtails. Immediately I put my hand on
her inhaler again. But Stephie giggled at the

149

Frankenstein, even though he didn't change the horrible expression on his face.

"He pulled my plait!" said Stephie in delight. "He must like me!"

(I loosened my grip on the inhaler.)

After waiting for fifteen minutes or so (and I must say that Stephie was a much more patient waiter than either Erick or Ryan), we boarded the tram. The seats were six across in each row.

"Ooh, can I sit on the end?" asked Stephie excitedly. (She had just spotted Frankenstein lurching around the tram. I think she was hoping for another pigtail-pull.)

"Of course," I said.

Erick and Ryan weren't happy. Kristy had made them sit in the middle two seats.

"How come *she* gets to sit by the side?" whined Ryan.

"Yeah," added Erick.

Kristy and I exchanged a glance. *We* knew why, but we couldn't very well tell the kids that it was because we thought Stephie would be well behaved, but the boys needed supervision. Luckily, Frankenstein *did* come past then, and Erick whipped out his camera. All was forgotten.

Kristy and I exchanged another glance. This one meant, Whew!

When everyone was settled, our tour guide introduced himself and gave us warnings about

150

staying in our seats and keeping our hands *inside* the tram at all times. Stephie, who was resting the very tips of her fingers on the edge of the tram, immediately pulled her hand into her lap, looking guilty.

"Don't worry," I told her.

"Okay," she replied, but she was solemn and subdued throughout the film and the long demonstration of special effects. She was *interested*, but she was awfully quiet.

"Feeling okay?" I asked her as we left the special-effects stage and reclaimed our seats on the tram.

"I'm fine," she replied. And then she added, "Honest."

"Okay." (I wasn't reassured.)

However, once the tour got going, Stephie perked up.

The tour wasn't exactly restful, but Stephie loved everything. You wouldn't believe the things that happened on our ride. I can't remember the *order* in which things happened, but this is what went on:

We drove through a dark tunnel and suddenly, from below us, King Kong loomed up. He was awful-looking. Even some of the adults on the tour were scared. Something burst into flames (false ones, I hope), sirens were screaming, a helicopter smashed to the ground and . . . King Kong was on the loose. Stephie was literally face to face with him. She gripped my hand (I gripped the inhaler) but she just shrieked with delight, even when he opened his mouth and bared his yellow teeth. (By the way, I could swear he had banana-breath.) His hairy chest and blazing eyes were just inches from Stephie—and she was giggling!

On another part of the tour, the guide began saying something like, "For those of you who remember the TV show *McHale's Navy . . .*" (My friends and I looked at each other and shrugged. *McHale's Navy*? It must have been one of those shows our parents watched. Maybe even our grandparents.) "For those of you who remember *McHale's Navy*, here's where it was filmed. Remember all that water? Well, this is it." (We were driving past a pool of water the size of a small pond.) "Of course, we haven't filmed the show in years, so this is an unused—"

Whoosh! Bang! Whoosh! Bang!

In the pond, two somethings exploded loudly, spraying water into the air.

"Hmm, I suppose there are still a few undetonated bombs out there," said our tour guide, trying to look concerned and surprised.

I put my arm protectively around Stephie in case another bomb should go off, but Stephie had loved the excitement.

"Great!" she said.

At another point on the ride, our guide was

152

talking away again. "Here we are, approaching this little Mexican village that we've used as a backdrop in many films. Isn't it nice that you see it when the sun is shining and . . . Uh-oh! What's that? I thought I heard thunder. And is that rain?"

Before I knew what was happening, a flood of water was rushing down a hill towards us and the tour guide was crying, "Look out! it's a flash flood!"

Of course it wasn't real, and of course Stephie loved it. As we drove away, I looked back. The water was already receding. How did they do that? I suppose it's the magic of film-making.

Okay. Then there was *Jaws*. I haven't seen the film because my father won't let me, but I know what it's about—a shark named Bruce (I don't know why that's his name) with an appetite for humans. I was pretty sure that as soon as our tour guide said, "And this is where *Jaws* was filmed," we were going to see Bruce. I was right. We saw him in a big way. First from across the lake—just his fin streaking through the water. Then the fin disappeared and the next thing I knew, Bruce was leaping out of the water, and like King Kong, he was just inches away from the tram. His gaping mouth, which was *filled* with fangs, was snapping viciously.

Stephie screeched, I grabbed her inhaler, and she exclaimed, "Awesome!"

153

Mary Anne

The last tunnel we drove through looked innocent enough in the beginning, but by now I knew better. What were we in for this time?

The walls were blue and white and we drove through the tunnel slowly. Then our tour guide said, "Well, here we are in the ice tunnel, the only way back to civilization. We should be safe—"

Of course we weren't. I heard a thundering noise and suddenly we were spinning around and around. "Avalanche!" cried the tour guide.

"Oh, my lord!" exclaimed Claud.

I clung to Stephie for dear life. If she fell out of the tram, her father would kill me. And why were there no seat belts in the tram? If we were going to go on a ride like this, we ought to be strapped in as if we were on a roller coaster.

I began to feel awfully sick and was glad we hadn't eaten lunch yet. I know my face must have been green, so I turned to look at Stephie. I hoped she didn't have a delicate stomach. But, as usual, Stephie was grinning away. Then she tugged at my sleeve.

"What? What is it? Do you need your inhaler?" I asked frantically.

"No!" Stephie was giggling. "Look! *We're* not turning, the walls of the tunnel are. We're staying completely still."

I looked. She was right. It was an optical illusion. I loosened my grip on Stephie, feeling pretty foolish. I also felt relieved. Lisa Meri and

154

the members of the We ♥ Kids Club had been right. Stephie's asthma attacks weren't brought on by activity or excitement.

I relaxed. And when the tram ride was over, I didn't worry about Stephie all afternoon. We saw a show called "Star Trek Adventure", we ate lunch (everyone found food they liked), and then we went to the Animal Actor's Stage, where we saw all kinds of animals do all kinds of tricks. Stephie especially liked the performing monkeys and giggled helplessly. After that, Jeff, Ryan, and Erick wanted to go and see a show about Conan, but Mr Schafer said we had to go home. So we went back to the car.

Stephie slept during the entire ride home. I knew I didn't have to worry about her any more.

                                                    Tuesday
Dear Claudia,
    How is everything going in California ? Have you been
to Universal Studios yet ? It sounds quite interesting.
I would especially like to learn about special effects. You
can tell me everything when you come home !
    Right now I am working on a physics project.
It is for extra marks for when school starts again.
Wish me luck.
                                    Love,
                                        Janine

Miss Claudia Kishi
c/o The Schafers

22 Buena Vista

Palo City, Ca. 92800

16th CHAPTER

Claudia

Wish her luck? Janine doesn't need luck with anything. She's a genius, remember? *I'm* the one who needs luck.

Today, when we were at Universal Studios, Stacey was on my back nonstop about Terry. (Well, whenever she wasn't helping Kristy to control Erick or Ryan.)

"You *can't* give up on him," she kept saying to me.

"But at dinner I gabbled on and choked on slugs—"

"Snails," corrected Stacey. "*Escargots*."

"Whatever. And I know I made a fool of myself."

"How do you know?" asked Stacey. (We were in the tunnel with King Kong and she wasn't paying attention to anything, including the giant gorilla.)

"Because . . . because . . ." I stammered.

"Did he stop talking to you? Did he roll his eyes at you?"

"No."

"So okay. Who knows what he thinks? Maybe he was impressed by you. *I'd* be impressed by anyone who ate snails."

"Oh, you don't understand," I muttered, as we left King Kong behind.

"Maybe not," said Stacey. "But you should give him another chance."

I thought about Stacey's words off and on during the rest of the afternoon. Maybe she was right. Maybe I shouldn't give up on Terry. So you know what I did when I got home that night?

I rang Janine . . . *Janine*!

This is why: I wanted to ask her about world affairs.

"World affairs?" repeated Janine.

"Yes. You know, like greenhouses and stuff."

"Do you mean Greenpeace? or the green-house effect?"

"Anything," I said. "I know there are things going on in Russia and—and in other countries. And some wall came down."

"Claudia, you're on holiday," said my sister. "Why do you need to know these things? It seems quite odd."

"I need to know them," I said, sighing, "to impress a boy. A really clever boy I met on the beach. He reads books like yours. And he speaks French."

"But Claudia, trying to impress him isn't going to help anything. Trust me. Sooner or later, he'll find out you're not who he thinks you are."

"Then what am I supposed to do?" I wailed. I felt a little funny talking to my sister like this. Usually we just talk about . . . well, I don't even know what. But not personal things.

"Just . . . be . . . yourself," said Janine.

I was silent for a few moments. At last I said, "That's what Dawn told me to do. I suppose I didn't listen to her."

"She gave you sound advice," said Janine wisely.

"Okay. But how am I supposed to be myself? That's harder to do than it sounds."

"Well," said Janine slowly, "what are you and your friends doing tomorrow?"

"Tomorrow? We're going to Hollywood. There's tons of stuff to do there."

"Why don't you ask Terry to join you? Could you do that?"

"I'm sure Dawn's father would say he could come. But the things to do in Hollywood . . . well, I don't think they would interest Terry. He likes books and reading and, um, current affairs."

"And what are you going to do in Hollywood?"

"Oh, see stars' homes and go to Grauman's Chinese Theatre. That kind of thing."

"How do you know Terry won't want to go along with you? *I* would. It sounds like a fun day."

"*You'd* want to drive around and try to find Cher's house?" I exclaimed.

"Yes. Why not?"

"I don't know. Okay. Maybe I will ask Terry to come with us tomorrow."

"Good! Let me know what happens."

"All right. And Janine?"

"Yes?"

"Thanks."

"You're welcome."

We rang off, and I felt pretty close to my sister, even though she was three thousand miles away. I also decided to take her advice. I asked Mr Schafer if Terry could come with us to Hollywood the next day. He said yes. So, with shaking hands, I dialled Terry's number.

Terry answered the phone.

Okay. Now I had to go through with this thing.

"Hi, Terry. It's Claudia," I began.

"Claudia! Hi!" (At least Terry seemed pleased to hear from me.)

"Um, I was wondering something. Of course, you don't have to do this if you don't want to. It's just an idea. I mean, it probably isn't the kind of

161

thing you like to do at all, but I thought I'd ask anyway. Remember, though, you don't have to do this. Don't feel pressured to—"

"Claudia, what *is* it?" Terry sounded tortured.

"Well, tomorrow, Mr Schafer is driving my friends and me to Hollywood. We're going to—you know—"

"Look for film stars' homes?" asked Terry.

"Yes."

"Go to the wax museum?"

"Maybe."

"Hmm."

I couldn't believe it. Now Terry sounded interested. "You mean you want to come with us? To Grauman's and places like that?"

"Definitely! I *love* old films. I like anything that has to do with stars."

"You're kidding! Why didn't you ever say so?"

"I don't know. I suppose the subject didn't come up."

"Oh." (Why hadn't I *brought* it up, instead of things I didn't know about?)

"When are we leaving?" asked Terry.

"We'll pick you up at eight-thirty tomorrow morning, okay?"

"Great! I can't wait."

"Me neither. I'll see you tomorrow. Oh, and don't get dressed up. We're all just wearing jeans and things."

162

"Okay. Goodnight, Claud. Hey, and thank you!"

Nervous wreck? Nervous *wreck*? Was I a nervous wreck the next day?

Definitely.

Our crowded van picked up Terry at eight-thirty on the dot. He was dressed casually, but with style. I think that's safe to say. He climbed into the van and sat next to me.

"Hi," we both said nervously.

I saw Kristy and Mary Anne elbow each other.

During the drive to Hollywood, Terry was pretty quiet, but maybe that was because he was squashed in with seven females. (Carol wasn't there, to Dawn's delight.) The only males were a kid and a grown-up. Uh-oh! I thought. We aren't even making small talk. I was chatting with the BSC members instead of Terry.

Finally we arrived in Hollywood. Mr Schafer parked the car. "We'll do a little walking today," he said. "How about starting at Grauman's Chinese Theatre?"

"Oh, boy!" said Mal. "I want to see how my feet compare with Marilyn Monroe's!"

Before we knew it, we were standing in front of a building with all these footprints in the cement on the pavement. We didn't pay a bit of attention to the building, but we ran around looking for footprints and sometimes trying to fit our feet into them. Terry was a bit reserved, but he did step into John Wayne's footprints (cowboy boot prints, actually.)

Next we walked past Hollywood High, where a lot of people who are stars now once went to school. Then we walked back to the street Grauman's is on and took a stroll down the Walk of Fame. It's a pavement studded with squares outlined in brass, and inside each star is the name of a famous personality. It's supposed to be a great honour to be on the Walk of Fame. But guess what Terry said? You have to *pay* to get a square in the pavement. And you have to pay a *lot* of money.

"How do you know?" I asked Terry.

"I just do," he replied. He smiled at me. And then he took my hand.

(Jeff sniggered.)

Terry held my hand as we bought a map of the stars' homes, got back in the van, and prepared to cruise around and see where famous people live (or lived). We drove all over the place. At first we were just awed. "That's Steve Martin's house?" "That's where Fred Astaire used to live?" "Oh, my lord! There's Harrison Ford's house!"

We grew more and more excited, but guess who was the most excited of all? Terry. Only he was impressed by people I'd never heard of, like Cornell Wilde, Anne Bancroft, and some others I can't remember.

I realized I was starving then, so I was really glad when Mr Schafer said, "How about lunch, everybody?"

"Great. I'm famished," replied Dawn.

"I wish the Brown Derby were still open," said Mary Anne. "We'd be bound to see stars there."

"We might see stars anywhere," said Terry excitedly.

So we found this nice restaurant full of little tables. Since the tables were so small, Terry and I sat at one alone together. We talked and talked. Terry told me how he had got so interested in films and film stars. Then I told him about the things that interest me. I told him about my art, I told him about the Babysitters Club, and I even told him about my grandmother Mimi, who had died. Terry liked hearing about the art the most, and was especially interested in a portrait of Mimi that I had painted.

When our day was over, I was actually sad. I realized that I wanted to keep seeing Terry. Why did such a great guy have to live in California when I live in Connecticut? Oh, well. There was nothing we could do about that.

But before Terry jumped out of the van he kissed me goodbye.

Monday

Dear Mum, Dad,
and Aunt Cecelia,
        Yesterday we went
to Hollywood! We drove
around and saw some
stars' homes. We saw
Steve Martin's house
and Bette Midler's
house, and even the
house where Fred
Astaire used to live.
Sometimes I think
maybe I should have
taken tap dancing
instead of ballet. My
goal would be to
dance as well as Fred.
        Lots of Love,
        Jessi

The Ramseys

612 Fawcett Avenue

Stoneybrook, Ct. 06800

17th
CHAPTER

Jessi

Hmm. Mallory and I had never been angry with each other in all the time we'd been best friends. We'd never even had an argument. But we were definitely having problems now. (Did I write that in the postcard to my parents and Aunt Cecelia? Of course not.) However, I wanted to straighten things out with my best friend.

So on Sunday night, after our trip to Hollywood, I sat down to think about what exactly was wrong between Mal and me. Straight away, I realized something important. Any argument takes two people, so Mal and I were both at fault. Mal was being *insufferable* about this business with her hair and make-up. (Everyone agreed to that.) And I was angry with her. I was angry with her for doing something she knew her parents wouldn't allow if they were around. And I was angry with her for spending all her money and expecting to borrow from me for the rest of the trip. I was also angry with *me* for not being more gracious about lending her the money. If I were out of money, Mal would let me borrow from her.

In fact, the more I looked at things, the more our problems seemed rather like my fault. So I decided to be the one to patch up our differences.

Trying very hard to ignore Mallory's blonde hair and seventy-five pounds of make-up, I said to her after dinner on Sunday, "Hey, Mal. Come outside with me for a minute, okay?"

"Okay, but why?"

"I just want to talk to you, that's all." And then I whispered, "In private."

Mallory looked alarmed and I couldn't blame her. She probably thought I was going to yell at her again for dyeing her hair or borrowing money. But she followed me bravely outside.

"I want to know—" I began.

"Yes?" said Mal in a trembly voice.

"If you'd like to come with me to watch Derek tomorrow." Mallory let out just about all the breath in her body, like a balloon deflating. She must have been *really* nervous. "Derek invited me back to the set of *P.S. 162*," I went on, "and I said I'd go. So—do you want to come?"

"Of course!"

"The reason I had to ask you in private is

because Derek said it would be all right for one other person to come with me, but that's all. I didn't want to hurt anyone's feelings. We'll just tell the others that Mr Masters invited you and me to the set. Okay?"

"Okay," said Mal. Then she added, "Gosh, I'd better look my best tomorrow."

Uh-oh! I knew what that meant. But I kept my mouth shut. Especially since Mal glanced uncertainly at me as soon as she said that.

We were still on shaky ground.

And I had to admit that I wasn't as excited about going to the TV studio the next day as I had been the week before. I knew Derek was going to ask me whether I'd looked into agents and things like that, and of course I hadn't. I hadn't done a thing about becoming a film star. I'd been thinking about it and remembering the crowd scene I'd been in. It had been fun—but only at first. I didn't like shooting and then reshooting and reshooting and reshooting. And I missed ballet. I missed practising at my *barre* in our basement.

Anyway, how could I live in L.A. when my home is in Stoneybrook? So I wasn't thrilled about Monday's plans, but I couldn't change them. I knew Mal wanted to get inside a TV studio, and I *did* want to say goodbye to Derek.

Early on Monday morning Mr Masters picked up Mal and me just like before. And just like before, we dropped Todd off at the nursery on the way to the studio. This time, I had to say goodbye to Todd, and he cried a little.

"I'll see you the next time you're back in Stoneybrook, okay?" I said.

"Okay," replied Todd, sniffling.

I gave him a hug before we drove off.

When we arrived at the studio, Mr Masters dropped off Derek and Mal and me so he could park the car.

As Derek led us inside, he said, "Today should be more interesting. I mean, more interesting than when you were here before, Jessi. We'll be doing more filming. And more rehearsing on stage."

"Filming?" repeated Mal. She patted her hair. "Do you think they might need extras again?"

"Don't know," replied Derek. He opened the door to the *P.S. 162* studio, and Mal and I followed him inside. It was already a hive of activity.

"Ooh," said Mal. "Look! Look over there! It's the girl who plays Charlene. And there's what's-her-name, who plays Danielle."

Mal gasped. "And there's George Aylesworth, one of the teachers!" Mal was *not* keeping her voice down.

"Shh!" I reminded her quietly.

"Guess what?" said Derek. "Today we start working with a special guest star."

Mallory's eyes widened. "*Who?*"

172

"Elaine Stritch."

Mal and I must have looked puzzled, because Derek said, "She used to be on Broadway all the time. And she's been in a Woody Allen film." (Obviously Derek knew more about such things than we did.)

"I bet Terry would know who she is," I said. "Do you think we could get her autograph?" I turned to Mal. "Then we could give it to Claud and she could give it to Terry. I bet he'd love it."

"I'll get her autograph today," said Derek confidently.

"Wow, thanks!" I said.

Just then, Derek was called away to start rehearsing, and Mr Masters arrived. He and Mal and I sat quietly, slightly apart from the action. But Mal couldn't stop talking. (At least she was whispering.)

"I can't believe all those cameras," she said. "I've never seen so much equipment in my life. And look—microphones hanging from the ceiling. Hey, what's the man doing on the stage?"

"It's not called a stage," I was able to say proudly. "It's called a set. And that man's the set dresser."

"The set dresser?"

"Yes. He's responsible for making sure each scene— each set—looks just the way it's supposed to look. And see that woman over there? Well, she's the person in charge of . . ."

173

I could have gone on forever, telling Mal all the technical things I'd learned from Derek, but suddenly someone yelled, "Quiet!"

We shut up. For the next few hours, Mr Masters, Mal and I watched Derek and his fellow actors and actresses, including the one named Elaine Stritch, rehearse and rehearse. The cameras were rolling, but the director kept yelling, "Cut!" Then everyone would have to start again.

"Hard work," Mal whispered to me so quietly I could barely hear her.

I just nodded.

The day went on. Sandwiches were brought in for lunch. Derek went to school for a few hours. When he returned, early in the afternoon, guess what happened? The director said he needed extras for another crowd scene.

"Oh, *wow*!" exclaimed Mal. "Come on, Jessi."

I shook my head. I'd made my decision about acting.

I was a dancer.

But Mal ran to the director. "I'll be in the scene!" she said.

The director gazed at her. At last he said, "Sorry. I'd like to let you in this scene, but your looks aren't quite right."

Mal just stared at him. Then she returned to me, crestfallen. "He said my looks aren't right. How could he mean that? I've never looked better. I'm a California girl."

174

It wasn't the right time to tell Mal that that phrase has absolutely no meaning, so instead, I just put my arm around her for a moment. We spent the rest of the afternoon watching the shooting. When the long day was over, Mr Masters and Derek dropped Mal and me off at Dawn's house. I said goodbye to Derek and told him my decision about ballet. He just shrugged. Then I made him promise that he'd call the next time he was in Stoneybrook, and Mal and I thanked Mr Masters for our wonderful day. (Well, it had been wonderful for me. I'd even got Elaine Stritch's autograph to give Claud to give Terry.) Mal didn't look too happy, though.

I walked into Dawn's house, vowing to do stretching exercises so I'd be ready for ballet class when I got back to Connecticut.

Monday

Dear Ben,

By the time you get this card I may be back in Stoneybrook. Who knows? Who cares? You'll never believe the humiliating thing that happened to me today. After all my work to change my appearance, I had a chance to be in a crowd scene in P.S. 162, and you know what the director said? He said my looks weren't right. I was shocked. What could he mean?

I am so depressed.

Love, Mal

Ben Hobart

59 Bradford Court

Stoneybrook, CT 06800

18th CHAPTER

Mallory

Ben Hobart is my boyfriend, sort of. What I mean is, we're just getting to be boyfriend and girl-friend. I'd written Ben a lot of postcards and letters while I was away, so he knew about my hair and things. I thought he'd be understanding—but he's a boy, so I wasn't sure.

That evening, Jessi seemed more like the Jessi I remembered. She spent about an hour stretching and pointing her toes and so on. I guessed it was back to ballet for her. Jessi is so clever. She's practically got a career cut out for her, and she doesn't do things like . . . well, like I'd done on the trip. She'd kept her head. She hadn't spent every penny of her money.

And she's beautiful. *She* doesn't have to worry about her looks.

I sat on the sofa in the Schafers' family room and watched Jessi work out (which, by the way, she was doing in her swimsuit, since she hadn't brought her leotard with her).

While Jessi practised I sat—and sighed. I sighed so many times that Jessi finally stopped what she was doing and said, "What's wrong, Mal?"

"I—I'm sorry, Jessi," I replied. "I know I've been a pain all week. It was stupid to waste my money on hair dye and make-up. And it wasn't right to expect to borrow money from you for the rest of the trip."

Jessi sat next to me on the sofa. "I'm sorry too," she said. "Really sorry. I shouldn't have given you such a hard time about your hair and everything. I mean, I'm not your mother. And I could have been nicer about the money. I just thought you were getting a little carried away."

"You know," I said, "we've never argued before."

"I know. I was thinking about that earlier."

"Let's try not to fight any more, okay?"

"Definitely!" agreed Jessi.

"We need each other too much," I added. "What would I do without you? What would you do without me? We're best friends."

"Oh," groaned Jessi. "You sound like a cheap greetings card."

We giggled. Then Jessi said, "I've got to get

179

back to my stretching. If Madame Noelle finds me out of shape when classes begin, she'll kill me."

So Jessi went back to stretching, and I went back to moping. I sat on the couch and hugged my knees to my chest. Every now and then, I cried a little. A tear would come to my eye and I'd let it trickle down my cheek, not even bothering to brush it away.

A while later, Stacey bounced into the family room. "Guess what!" she cried. "We've just found out that there's a cinema nearby that only shows *old* films, and you won't believe what's playing tonight."

"What?" asked Jessi, standing up straight.

"*Mary Poppins!*" (*Mary Poppins* is Stacey's favourite film.) "So we're all going to go, okay? We're leaving right now."

"Terrific," exclaimed Jessi. "Just let me put on some decent clothes."

"Mal?" said Stacey questioningly.

I stayed in my curled-up position and just shook my head.

"What's wrong with her?" Stacey asked Jessi.

"I'll explain on the way to the film," Jessi whispered.

My friends left.

All evening I moped alone. And since I didn't feel like talking to anyone, I made sure I was in my sleeping bag by the time the other BSC members returned from the film.

The next day, I awoke to the sound of Mary Anne saying, "Let's go to Knott's Berry Farm today!"

"The amusement park?" said Claud. "Yes, lets! That might be fun. Dawn, have you already been there a million times?"

"No. Just twice," she replied. "And I know there's at least one new attraction since the last time I was there. A water ride, I think, so we should bring our swimsuits. And you can pan for gold—real gold—and see a dolphin show, and there are tons of rides. I'm going!"

"So am I," said Jessi.

"Me, too," added Stacey, Claud, Kristy, and of course Mary Anne.

"Mal?" asked Dawn.

I sighed. "I think I'll stay at home and read today."

Since I was lying on my stomach, with my head buried in my pillow, I don't know what my friends' reactions to this statement were, but I bet they were exchanging a lot of Looks.

So I spent Tuesday morning and most of the afternoon continuing to mope around Dawn's house. I did read a little, but mostly I felt incredibly sorry for myself. I looked in the

181

bathroom mirror about ninety-five times. "You're ugly," I said. "You're a toad."

"What did you say?"

I jumped a mile. Kristy had appeared in the mirror behind me. The girls had returned, and I'd been so busy being depressed that I hadn't heard them come in.

I whirled around. "Kristy, you scared me to death."

"You're pretty scary yourself, Mallory. What do you mean you're a toad?"

I thought about listing all the things that were wrong with me. Instead, I just wandered back to the family room and sank onto the sofa.

"Mal? Are you ill?" asked Dawn. The other girls were filtering inside.

"No, she's not," Kristy answered for me. "She's being a pain."

"Kristy!" exclaimed Mary Anne.

"Well, she is," said Kristy. "She's been moping around for almost twenty-four hours just because some guy told her she doesn't have the right look. Well, of course she doesn't. She doesn't look like herself. She's trying to look like someone she isn't. Tell me, Mallory, has your blonde hair or your make-up made a bit of difference in your life?"

I shook my head miserably.

"Well, then," Kristy went on (and by now all the BSC members were in the family room, listening to Kristy and me and Kristy's big mouth), "I'm going to say here and now that I liked the old Mal a lot better."

"Yes?" I said.

Kristy was cringing a little, but when I didn't blow up at her, my other friends started speaking up, too. They all agreed with Kristy. And Jessi said, "Mal? Would you go back to your old redheaded, make-up free self?"

I nodded. "But it isn't going to be easy," I added. "This shampoo-out dye doesn't just wash out. I mean, it will come out eventually, but only after a lot of washings. What am I going to do? I can't go home as a blonde."

To their credit, nobody said anything like, "Well, you should have thought of that before you blew all your money." Instead, Stacey said, "Then there's just one solution. You'll have to dye your hair red again."

"Huh?"

"We'll go to a chemist, we'll look very carefully for the exact colour your hair *really* is, and then you'll dye it red. If we match it up right, as the dyed hair grows out, nobody should be able to tell the difference between that and your natural hair. Okay?"

"Okay," I replied. I was only just beginning to realize the trouble I was in. (Or might be in if things didn't go well.)

There were still a couple of hours left until dinner, so the seven of us set off for a chemist that isn't too far from Dawn's house. We walked inside, asked the first salesperson we saw where the hair dye was (she gave us a suspicious look), and she pointed us to aisle three.

Can you believe it? Aisle three was *all* hair dye. Shelves and shelves of different brands and different shades. Some of the shades appeared almost the same, at least on the box covers. How would I ever find my *exact* colour. My friends must have been wondering the same thing because they looked awfully confused.

"Oh, my lord!" muttered Claud.

"Now just calm down, all of you," said Stacey. "Everybody concentrate. Close your eyes, try to imagine Mallory's hair colour, and then go and find a box that matches that colour."

So we did. We came back with seven different boxes. However, they were pretty close in colour, and after a *lot* of discussion, we finally chose one box.

Jessi bought it for me.

That night I dyed my hair again. It was a rather long process and everybody waited nervously to see what the final result would be. When I'd finished, I unwrapped the towel from around my head.

"Well?" I said.

I heard six sighs of relief.

"It's you again," said Jessi simply.

"Thank goodness. I suppose I'm a Connecticut girl after all."

"What about your make-up?" asked Jessi.

"Hey!" cried Stacey. "I've got a great idea. Claudia and I will buy it from you. Is that okay? *We* use make-up."

"*Okay*! It's great!" I exclaimed.

So I gave my make-up to Stacey and Claud and they gave me some money, and I gave the money to Jessi. "Now I only owe you a little," I said happily.

The next day, my friends and I went off in separate directions. Dawn stayed at home with her father and Jeff; Stacey went surfing (of course); Kristy, Mary Anne, and Claudia went to a double programme at the cinema they'd discovered; and Jessi and I just decided to walk around the neighbourhood. We were in the park where Mary Anne had taken Stephie, when Jessi nudged me.

"That boy's staring at you!" she whispered. "Turn *very slowly* to your left. Don't be obvious."

I turned. A nice boy about my age *was* staring at me. He smiled. I smiled back.

"Wow!" I said to Jessi, as we walked along. I was flattered. A boy had noticed me— and real me—and smiled.

But Ben Hobart was waiting for me back in Stoneybrook.

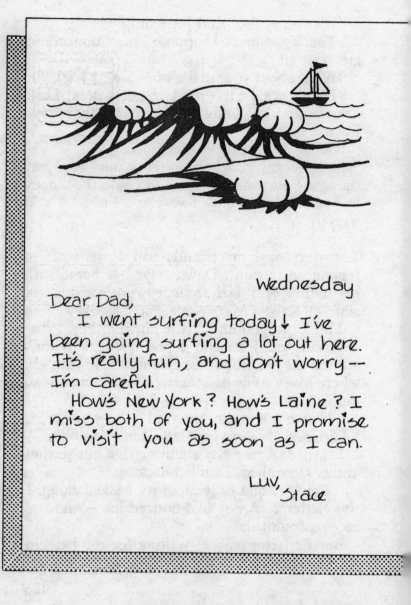

Wednesday

Dear Dad,
 I went surfing today! I've been going surfing a lot out here. It's really fun, and don't worry— I'm careful.
 How's New York? How's Laine? I miss both of you, and I promise to visit you as soon as I can.

LUV,
Stace

Mr Edward McGill

321 East 65th St. Apt. 2F

New York, NY 10000

19th CHAPTER

Stacey

I think we were all editing our postcards, some of us more than others. This particular postcard left out every single important thing that happened on Wednesday. In fact, it didn't say much at all. And I can prove it. This is what *really* happened on Wednesday:

Early in the morning (well, not *too* early) my surfing friends dropped by to pick me up. Beau was at the wheel again, which gave me sort of a thrill. I knew the rides to and from the beach would be exciting.

And they were.

Especially the ride home. After a day of surfing we were tired—very tired.

"I just want to get *home*," said Beau, as he climbed into the car. Paul and Alana sat in the

188

front with him, and Carter, Rosemary, the surfboards, and I were crammed into the back.

Beau pulled out of the beach car park. He
pulled out so fast that Paul said, "Hey, slow
down." I'd never heard Paul talk to Beau like
that, especially considering that Paul does a fair
amount of speeding himself.

Anyway, it was a good thing we *had* pulled out
fast, because Beau had turned right in front of an
oncoming car. If he'd been driving any slower, we
would have been hit. I decided Beau was a good
driver who knew what he was doing.

I told him so.

"I'm an aggressive driver," he replied proudly.

I wasn't sure what that was, but since Beau
sounded so proud, I said, "That's great. Driving
with you is exciting."

We'd been on the motorway for a little while
when Beau, who was in the middle of three lanes,
said, "If we stay behind this lorry any longer, we
won't get home until next week. That driver must
be the slowest guy in California."

Now, I don't know a *lot* about driving, but I do
know, from watching my parents, that when you
want to make a turn or switch into another lane,
you put on your indicator. But Beau just made
that remark about being the slowest driver in
California and zoomed into the left lane—the
fastest one—without putting on his indicator,
checking the mirrors, or anything. "Jerk!" he

muttered to the guy in the lorry as he pulled out.

The next thing I knew, I heard an amazing crunch of metal and wondered what could possibly have happened. It sounded like the time when I was living in New York and a crane fell onto a car.

The crunch was just a distraction for a half a second. That was how long it took me to realize that *our* car had been crunched. After that, everything seemed to happen in slow motion. The car in the left lane that Beau had sideswiped skidded into the crash barrier. The car behind that one smashed into the back of it. And our car was bounced in the other direction like a ping-pong ball—right into the side of the lorry, and both our car and the lorry skidded to the opposite side of the motorway and into the crash barrier. Luckily no one behind smashed into *us*.

I was aware of the sound of breaking glass (the lorry's), and of being wrenched first sideways and then forward. If I hadn't been wearing my seat belt, I don't know what would have happened. As it was, I thought I could feel every single bone in my body rattle.

And then time seemed to stop. I could hear cars on the motorway either going around us, or trying to stop in front of us—I suppose to help. Then I think I might have fainted or something because the next thing I knew, Rosemary was shaking my arm and crying, "Stacey! Stacey!" over and over again. She sounded alarmed.

"Yes?" I replied.

"Oh, thank goodness," said Rosemary. "Come on. We've got to get out of here."

"Why?" I asked, feeling as if I'd just woken from a long sleep.

"*Because*. We can't stay in the car. What if someone else runs into us? Besides, the car could blow up or something."

I started to open the car door.

"Unbuckle your seat belt," said Rosemary impatiently.

I did so. Then I tried the door again. I couldn't budge it. My head was clearing and I looked over the edge of the car. "We're stuck to the crash barrier," I announced.

"Oh, great!" said Beau sarcastically, and for the first time I began to wonder if everyone else was okay. And how the people in the other cars were.

"Is anyone hurt?" I cried, and I knew I sounded hysterical.

"Just cuts and bruises," replied Paul from the front seat. "Stacey, are you *sure* you can't open your door?"

"Positive. What about you?"

"I've tried. Beau, maybe if you could just pull up a few inches?"

"Pull *up*? I can't even start the car. We'll just climb out."

It was at that moment that we heard sirens.

191

"Oh," groaned Beau. "I'm in for it now." He paused. "Hey, listen, all of you. Will you back me up? Will you say that the lorry put on its brakes suddenly and I had to swerve to go around him? That's why I pulled into the left lane so fast."

"Of course," said everyone except Paul and me.

I wasn't about to lie. And I was surprised to hear Paul ask, "Before we got caught behind the lorry, Beau, how fast were you driving?"

"Oh, about seventy-five, maybe eighty."

Paul shook his head. Carter and Rosemary exchanged a glance.

The siren we had heard slowed down behind us. The next thing I knew, a police officer was standing over Beau. "Anyone in here seriously hurt?" he asked.

"No," we replied.

"Okay. Out of the car."

Out of the car? I couldn't get out on my side. There was a sharp drop just beyond the crash barriers. And on the other side of the car was the motorway. How would we get out with all those cars whizzing by? That was when I realized there *were* no cars whizzing by. The police must have put up a roadblock or created a detour or something. They worked really fast.

Anyway, what I saw as I slid across the seat and climbed outside I can only describe as an accident scene: three crushed cars and a crushed lorry, ambulances and a fire engine screaming to a halt, and about a thousand police cars. Officers were milling around everywhere. I heard one of them say, "Amazing. No one's badly hurt."

Some of the police officers were walking around with pads of paper, asking questions. When a young woman stepped up to me, wanting to know what had happened, I told her the truth.

Beau gave me a look that could have killed a snake.

I began to feel shaky—very frightened all of a sudden. I suppose I'd just realized what might have happened, how bad the accident could have been. I slumped to the pavement, leaned against Beau's car, and began to cry. For that reason, I was the first person put into an ambulance and driven to a nearby hospital. (Eventually everyone, hurt or not, arrived at the hospital.)

At the hospital, a casualty doctor checked me over carefully.

"I'm fine, I'm fine," I kept telling her.

"We're just making sure," she replied. "Sometimes injuries don't show up right away, and you're pretty shaky." But finally she pronounced me ready to leave. "You're going to be sore tomorrow," she warned me, "and you may find some bruises, but otherwise you're okay. And you're very lucky," she added.

"I know," I replied.

193

"Okay. Who are you going to ring to come pick you up?"

"My friend's father," I told her. "I'm just visiting here."

I left to look for a pay phone. I found one in the lobby. I was glad that Carter and everyone were still in casualty, because they'd been giving me some pretty nasty looks. I knew I'd never see *them* again.

My shakiness returned as I dialled Dawn's number. What was her father going to say—or do? Would he make me ring my parents? Would he send me back to Stoneybrook early? I knew I'd been asking for trouble ever since I arrived in California, and now the trouble was here, and I was going to have to pay for it.

The phone rang at Dawn's house. And rang again. And then, guess who answered it? Carol! Oh, that was perfect. Carol was just like one of us. If *she* picked me up at the hospital, Mr Schafer might never even know about the accident.

"Hi, Carol," I said. "It's Stacey." When I told her where I was and what happened, she said that she and Dawn would be there as fast as they could. (Mr Schafer had taken Jeff out for a while.)

I sat in the waiting room of the hospital, feeling incredibly lucky. And when Dawn and Carol walked through the big double doors, I ran to them. Dawn hugged me. Carol hugged me, too.

But the first words out of her mouth were, "You know I'll have to tell Dawn's father about this, don't you?"

No. I didn't know. Apparently Dawn hadn't thought about it, either. She looked at me with eyes about the size of flying saucers.

The ride home was mostly silent. And when we reached Dawn's house, I was dismayed to see Mr Schafer's car in the drive. He was back from wherever he'd taken Jeff.

"Darling?" Carol called as soon as we entered the house. "We need to talk."

Mr Schafer hurried to the front door. "Is anything wrong?" he asked.

"Let's go somewhere private," said Carol. "Stacey has something to tell you."

We (Carol, Mr Schafer, Dawn, and I) went into the family room and closed the door. My other friends were around—I'd seen Claud and Mary Anne on my way in—and I was sure they knew something was up. I wished they could be with me then, but I knew that Mr Schafer wanted to handle this his own way.

The four of us sat down, Dawn and I together on the sofa, and Mr Schafer and Carol in armchairs.

"Okay, Stacey," said Carol. "Go ahead." (Her voice was gentle.)

I drew in a deep breath, then let it out slowly.

"Mr Schafer," I said, "I was in a car crash on the way home from the beach today."

Sunday

Hi Sweetie!

Richard and I really miss you and Mary Anne. The house is like a tomb at night. No loud music, no chattering, no friends dropping in. I know you're having fun on your trip, though. Say hi to your dad, and give Jeff a kiss for me (if he'll let you).

Lots of Love,
Mom

P.S. Tell Mary Anne that Tigger can't wait for her to come home.

Miss Dawn Schafer
22 Buena Vista
Palo City, CA   92800

20th CHAPTER

Dawn

"Dawn? Dawn?"

Bother. Carol was calling me. I'd come in from the warm sun, craving a glass of ice water, and now I had to face Carol.

"Yes?" I said. We met in the kitchen, where Carol was just putting down the phone.

"Dawn, sit down but don't worry," she said immediately.

Well, of course I was nearly out of my mind. No one likes to hear those words. But I sat and tried to look calm. I wasn't about to panic in front of Carol. "What's wrong?" I asked.

"That was Stacey. She was calling from the hospital. She was in a car accident on the way home from the beach," (I gasped) "but she's absolutely *fine*. Just a couple of bruises. Let's go and pick her up, okay?"

I was strapped into the front seat of Carol's car before Carol had even left the kitchen, and we got to the hospital in record time. When I saw Stacey just sitting in the waiting room, not covered with blood or anything, I ran to her and hugged her. Then Stacey and Carol hugged, and I was about to hug Carol, too, believe it or not, just because I was so relieved and everything. But that was when Carol said to Stacey, "You know I'll have to tell Dawn's father about this, don't you?" My jaw dropped. I couldn't believe it. I don't think Stacey could believe it, either. Carol had always tried so hard to be like one of us, and now she was acting like an adult.

Stacey, Carol, and I barely said a word on the ride home. I was fuming. Why couldn't Carol keep this a secret? All right Stacey *had* been hanging around with older kids, doing dangerous things, and now she'd been in a car accident, but she wasn't hurt. Anyway, we only had a few more days of holiday left. Stacey could just stay away from her surfing pals.

But no, Carol had to tell Dad right away. When the four of us sat down in the family room, I could actually feel the tension in the air.

Then Stacey said, "Mr Schafer, I was in a car crash on the way home from the beach today." My father turned slightly pale, but he just nodded. "Four cars got smashed up," Stacey went on. "No one was hurt—at least not badly—but the accident was caused by Beau. He was the driver of our car."

I was proud of Stacey. She went on to say how she'd found Beau and her other older friends and the car rides and the surfing pretty thrilling. But now she saw what danger she'd been in. Then she apologized—about thirty-six times.

Dad was silent for a long while. This wasn't a bad sign. It just meant that he was thinking. At last he said, "Stacey, I'm not your parent, but while you're staying with me, I'm responsible for you. So I have to forbid you to go anywhere with those kids or to see them again."

"Okay," said Stacey softly.

"Furthermore, I think we should phone your parents."

"My parents? No! Please!" cried Stacey.

And Carol spoke up then. "I really think we should," she said to Stacey. "Your parents have a right to know. Besides, you aren't hurt and you won't see those friends again. If you want, Dawn's dad and I can talk to them first, and then you can get on the phone to prove to them that you're okay."

I looked at Carol with some respect. And with even more respect when she went on to say, "I do hope you've learned something from this, Stacey."

Stacey reddened. But she said, "Yes. I have." Although she didn't say what.

So my father asked, "What have you learned?"

And Carol replied for Stacey. "I don't think she has to tell us. She knows what she's learned. Don't you, Stacey?"

"Yes," said Stacey, still red in the face.

We talked for a few minutes longer, and then Dad said, "Stacey, I'm really sorry that this happened, but I'm glad you're not hurt. Promise me you'll tell me if you feel any pain, or anything that's not quite right."

Stacey promised. Then she stayed with Dad and Carol to make the phone calls, while I left the family room.

When I opened the door to step out in the hall, I tripped over Jessi, Kristy, Claudia, Mary Anne, Mallory, and Jeff, all of whom were crowded in the hallway. They jumped back sheepishly.

"Come on. Let's go and talk in my room," I said.

We walked to my room in a crowd—including Jeff. I love my brother, but I had to tell him, as my friends filed past him into the bedroom, that he couldn't come in. "BSC members only," I said.

"Rats!" Jeff walked off in a huff.

I closed my door and we all found seats somewhere. For a few minutes, no one said anything. Then Stacey joined us and began to cry.

"I'm so embarrassed," she managed to say.

"It's okay, Stace," said Claudia soothingly. "You got carried away while you were out here. That's all."

"I'll say! My parents took the news pretty well, all things considered."

"You should be glad you were wearing your seat belt. Especially since you were in an open-top sports car. Try not to be embarrassed. We're just glad you're here." Claud looked a little weepy.

There was silence for a few moments. Then Stacey burst out, "I can't believe what Carol did. I thought she was our friend. She was always on our side, driving us to places, giving us advice about boys and things."

"I know," I said. "I was angry too. On the way home from the hospital, all I could think about was that she was going to tell my father. I really thought she'd keep it a secret. But then I started thinking about things. And *then* I listened to her when she and Dad and you and I were having our conversation. You know, it's one thing to talk to Carol about boy problems or make-up problems. It's another to keep something as major as the accident from my father or your parents, Stace. Carol can't cover up something like that. My father would never trust her again.

"And you know what else? Carol *is* older than we are. So she should act older. I liked her better tonight, when she was being a parent, than when

203

she was trying to be our friend or our older sister or something. She *ought* to act responsibly. After all, Dad puts her in charge of Jeff and me sometimes."

"That's true," agreed Mary Anne. "It would be like if we were babysitting and one of the kids broke something, or did something really bad. We would have to tell the parents. That's our responsibility as a sitter—as the person in charge."

"You're right," agreed Stacey. But she still looked as if she felt awful, and I'm sure she did. She was embarrassed, humiliated, and she was probably beginning to hurt. Already I could see a purple bruise on her arm.

When things had died down (and after Stacey climbed painfully into my bed—I wouldn't let her sleep in a sleeping bag that night), I found my father in the kitchen. Carol had gone and he was sitting at the table, reading the paper and drinking a cup of coffee.

"Dad?" I said. "Can we talk?"

"Of course, darling," he replied. He folded the newspaper and set it aside.

I had a big question on my mind, and I decided there was only one way to ask it—bluntly. "Are you going to marry Carol?" I wanted to know.

Dad stared into his coffee cup.

"I'm sorry," I said, feeling ashamed. "I suppose that was too personal."

"No, no. That's not it. I'm just not sure what the answer is. I like Carol—I *love* her," said my father. (I blushed, not used to hearing him talk that way.) "But I don't know if I'm ready to jump into another marriage. That means a lot of commitment. Also, you and Jeff don't seem too keen on Carol."

Now it was my turn to stare, only I didn't have a coffee cup to look into, so I stared at my hands, which were folded in my lap.

"Dawn?" said Dad.

"Just thinking," I replied. "I want to say this properly." I paused again. At last I said, "I didn't know Carol too well before. I mean, I've met her, but—you know— this holiday is the most time I've spent with her. And at first I didn't like her much. She drove Mal and Jessi to that beauty museum and she talked to Claudia about Terry. It was as though she was trying to be one of us. And she isn't. She's an adult. My friends and I are grown-up, and we're responsible and everything, but we're not adults like you and Carol. So then, do you know what? Since Carol had seemed so young, Stacey and I really thought she would keep the car accident a secret. When she said she wouldn't, I was furious, until I heard what she had to say when we were talking with you. I was—I felt—I don't know exactly . . .''

205

"Did you feel respect for her?" asked Dad gently.

"I suppose so," I replied. "Dad? If you want to marry Carol, I think it would be okay with me. I really do. Besides, it's *your* decision."

Dad got up from the table, came around to my side, and gave me a hug. Neither of us said a word. But when I left the kitchen, I went into the family room, shut the door for privacy, found a pen and a piece of stationery, and began a letter.

Dear Carol, it said. As soon as I'd written those words, I knew the rest were going to be tough. Tougher than an English composition. After a lot of thought, I started by saying that I was sorry I hadn't been very nice to her. I tried (diplomatically) to explain why. Then I said that I was glad she had told Dad about Stacey's accident, and that I understood that she'd had to do that. I even came right out and said that I liked her better when she acted like my mother than like my friend. Finally I told her I was really glad that my father had found someone he likes so much. I hoped they would be happy together. (I also hoped that last part was not too forward, since as far as I knew, Dad had not yet asked Carol to marry him.)

My next big decision was when to give Carol the letter. I decided to post it to her after I was back in Stoneybrook. I mean, if I couldn't *tell* her these things, how could I give her the letter before

206

Dawn

I left? We might have to talk, and I wasn't ready
for that.

But I was ready to accept Carol.

Thursday

Dear Dad and Sharon,
I'll probably get to
Stoneybrook before this
letter does, unless it travels
by jet!
We're still having a fine
time, but a really scary
thing happened today.
Don't worry. I wasn't in
any danger, but this little
girl I was sitting for was.
Everything turned out fine,
though. I'll tell you about
it when I see you.
    Love to you and, of course,
        Tigger,   MaryAnne

Mr and Mrs Richard Spier

177 Burnt Hill Road

Stoneybrook, Ct. 06800

21st
CHAPTER

Mary Anne

On Thursday, two days before we would have to return to the East Coast, I babysat for Stephie one last time. Lisa Meri was at Stephie's (as the morning babysitter), and Stephie ran to greet me. No more hiding in her room.

"Hi, Mary Anne!" she cried.

"Hiya!" I replied. (Lisa and I smiled at each other over Stephie's head.)

Ten minutes later, Lisa had left, and Stephie and I were wondering what to do. We were sitting in the kitchen and I was starting to prepare lunch.

"Wait!" said Stephie. "I know what we can do."

"What?" I asked.

"Let's go to the park and have another picnic

lunch, just like we did the first time you babysat for me."

"Great," I replied. What did I have to worry about now? Stephie had survived Frankenstein, King Kong, an earthquake, a collapsing bridge, and an avalanche that had fooled me, but not her. This time we could *really* play in the park. We could eat—and then Stephie could play on anything she wanted.

My fears about her were gone.

So we packed a picnic basket with sandwiches, pears, biscuits, and cartons of fruit juice. I remembered to put Stephie's inhaler and pills in my pocket, and we were off. As soon as we stepped out the front door, Stephie looked up at me, smiled, and took my hand.

As we walked down her front drive, though, her smile faded. "I wish you didn't have to go back to where you live," she said.

"I know. But I do have to go back. My dad and stepmother and kitten are there. They miss me and I miss them."

"*I'll* miss you when you're gone," said Stephie, her voice trembling.

"And I'll miss you."

Stephie tightened her grip on my hand as we reached the pavement. Was she going to cry? She'd seemed so happy a few moments earlier.

I soon had my answer. Tears were rolling down Stephie's cheeks.

"Oh, Stephie," I said. I put the picnic basket on the ground, knelt down, and hugged her while she cried silently. I didn't say, "Don't cry," because everyone has a right to cry when they're feeling bad. And I didn't say, "It's okay," because it wasn't. And I couldn't make it okay.

So I just held Stephie for as long as she needed to be held. If I had a mother, that's what I would have wanted her to do for me.

Just as I was thinking that, Stephie sniffled and said, "I wish you were my mother. I really do."

I smiled. "I'd be an awfully young mother," I pointed out. "I'm only thirteen. I would have had you when I was five."

I'd thought Stephie would laugh at that, but instead I heard her gasp.

"What's wrong?" I asked, pulling away from her. I thought she'd seen something scary, like a large dog or a spider.

But Stephie just gasped again. She began trying to breathe in big gulps of air. "I'm—I'm having an asthma attack!" she managed to say. She sounded panicky. (Well, of course she sounds panicky, stupid! I said to myself. She can't breathe. She must be scared to death.)

I fumbled for Stephie's inhaler. Why was she having an attack *now*? We weren't doing anything. And then I remembered what I'd learned about asthma. In Stephie's case, it was usually brought

212

on by emotional stress. I guessed my leaving was too much for her. I felt horrible.

But my feelings were not the problem.

The problem was that Stephie couldn't breathe.

I handed Stephie her inhaler. With one hand, she shook it. I held onto her other hand for comfort. Then I began to coach Stephie as I'd been coached. "Breathe *out*," I told her. (Stephie did so.) "Now put the short end of the inhaler into your mouth, push down, and breathe in deeply. Hold your breath for as long as you can . . . Good girl," I added, even though Stephie was choking. (Lisa Meri had told me that the inhaler works, but it isn't very pleasant.) "Now let your breath out slowly."

Stephie did, and she looked less panicky. I stroked her hair.

"Okay, now do that once more."

And Stephie followed my instructions, choking again. But when she let her breath out for the second time, she seemed fairly calm. And she was breathing again. But she was so weak that I had to pick her up and carry her back into her house, leaving the picnic basket on the pavement.

When we reached her front door, I opened it (with great difficulty) and laid Stephie on the living room couch. Then I dashed into the kitchen, got a glass of water, and handed it to Stephie, along with one of her pills.

"Here," I said. "Take this. It'll relax you and

you'll breathe even better." I held out the glass and the pill.

Stephie shook her head with tear-filled eyes.

"No?" I said. "But Stephie you *have* to. You know that. And I trust you to take it. So I'm going to leave you here with the pill while I go outside and bring the picnic basket in. Okay?"

"Okay."

I retrieved the basket. When I returned, the pill had gone, and the glass of water was only half full.

"Good girl," I told her.

"Thanks," said Stephie. She looked awfully pale and weak, but her breathing seemed normal.

"I'm going to make a quick phone call," I told her. "I'll be right back."

"You're not calling the hospital, are you?" cried Stephie, and I could hear a wheeze in her breathing.

"No. Calm down. Of course not. I just want to let your father know what happened. I don't want to surprise him when he comes home from work."

"Okay."

"Now *relax*."

"Okay." Stephie closed her eyes. The wheezing had stopped.

I dialled Mr Robertson at work. His phone number was stuck on the fridge with the emergency numbers. I reached his office and luckily Mr Robertson was available.

214

"Hi, this is Mary Anne Spier, Stephie's afternoon sitter."

"Oh! Yes. Is there a problem?" Mr Robertson sounded concerned.

"Stephie's just had an asthma attack," I told him. "But she's breathing fine now. She's resting on the sofa. She used her inhaler and she took a pill. I thought you'd want to know, even though there's nothing to worry about."

"Thank you. Thank you very much," said Mr Robertson. "Listen, make Stephie rest this afternoon—keep her on the sofa—and I'll try to come home early today. If she has *any* more trouble, call me right away." He paused. Then he added stiffly, "Tell Stephie I love her."

"I will," I replied.

When I returned to the living room, Stephie's eyes were closed, so I sat down quietly and picked up a magazine. But right away, Stephie said, "I'm awake," and opened her eyes.

I smiled. "Your dad says to tell you he loves you. He's going to try to come home early from the office today."

"Okay," said Stephie.

"So how are you feeling?"

"All right. Just tired."

"Yes. Your dad also said you have to rest all afternoon."

"Can we talk, though?" asked Stephie.

215

"Of course," I replied. "What do you want to talk about?"

"I don't know," said Stephie in a tone that I was sure meant she *did* know. I waited while Stephie gathered her thoughts. At last she said, "Tell me more about your father, Mary Anne."

"My father? Well, like I said, he used to be strict. And he treated me like a baby. Also, he was *really* over-protective. He wanted me to be perfect. I suppose so that he could show everyone that he could bring me up all right on his own."

"But something must have changed," said Stephie. "I mean you're *here*. He let you fly all the way to California."

"Well, actually two things changed. First when I was twelve, I was able to show my father how mature I really was. When he finally understood that I wasn't his little girl any more—that I could take care of some things by myself—he relaxed. And then he got married. To Dawn's mother! Mrs Schafer is my stepmother now, and she's *very* relaxed, so my dad relaxed with me even more."

"I wish I could show my dad that I'm grown up. But each time I have an asthma attack, it ruins everything. Then he thinks I'm someone who needs to be taken care of."

"That *is* a problem," I agreed, "but I bet you'll find some other way to show your dad that you're not a baby. It might take a while, though. You'll just have to be patient. After all, I had to wait until I was twelve."

Stephie sighed. Then she said, "You know what? I understand that you have to leave. I don't want you to go, but I know you have to."

"That's right," I said. "But just because I'm leaving and we're going to say goodbye today doesn't mean we can't keep in touch. It doesn't even mean I won't see you again. I might come out to visit the Schafers again. Don't forget Dawn and I are stepsisters."

"Can we be pen pals?" asked Stephie.

"Of course," I replied. "I love having pen pals. We can send each other letters and photos and stickers and postcards."

"Okay." Stephie smiled. "I'd like that."

Later in the day, Mr Robertson came home and I left. Stephie and I hugged, but we didn't cry.

We had already said our goodbyes.

Friday

Dear Granny and Pop-Pop,

I'm going to beat this card to Stoneybrook! In fact, I'll probably see you tomorrow, either at the airport or after Mum and Richard and Mary Anne and I get home.

Today is the last day of our holiday, which has been wonderful. We've done so many things. And of course it was great to see Jeff and Dad again. Today we are going to an amusement park called Six Flags Magic Mountain. Then we are going to have a really special dinner which I'll tell you about when I see you.

Lots of love,
Dawn

Granny and Pop-Pop Porter

747 Bertrand Drive

Stoneybrook, Ct. 06800

22nd
CHAPTER

Dawn

Well. Things certainly changed towards the end of the holiday. For one thing, the BSC seemed more like the BSC again. By that I mean that we were back to normal and we were hanging around as a group again. We didn't split up so often—and Stacey hadn't seen or heard from the surfers.

Mallory's hair was back to its original colour. At least, we thought it was the original colour. If it looked any different to her parents the next day, she could just tell them she'd spent a lot of time in the sun. (The only problem would be when the dyed part started to grow out. We just had to hope it wouldn't be *too* different from her natural colour.)

Mal and Jessi were best friends again, thank goodness. (I hate it when members of the BSC fall out with each other.) They apologized, Mal only owed Jessi a little money, since Claud and Stacey bought all of Mal's make-up from her. Of course, poor Mal didn't have any souvenirs of California, unless you count her hair. Also, Jessi had got the acting bug out of her system (again). Derek always seems to make her think of acting or modelling, Jessi gets excited, and then she realizes that ballet is her true calling.

Oh. Here's some big news: Claudia and Terry went out again. They went out last night (their final date) and Claud wasn't a bit nervous. She had her self-confidence back, at least with Terry. They went to see an old film (one Claud wanted to see), and then instead of going out for snails or fancy food, they went to Captain Rooster's Chicken Ranch for fried chicken, chips and stuff like that. Claudia practically floated through the Schafers' front door when Terry's mum dropped her off after the date.

"I'm in love," she said, and headed for her sleeping bag, even though it wasn't very late.

"Does love make you tired?" asked Mal innocently.

"No. I just want to dream about Terry all night."

Jessi and Mal looked perplexed. The rest of us exchanged smiles.

Kristy and Mary Anne's babysitting woes were over. I think Kristy learned a lesson: She's *not* the babysitting expert of the galaxy. And Mary Anne will miss Stephie, of course, but they promised to write to each other. Mary Anne admitted that she was relieved not to have to sit for Stephie again (the asthma attack was scary, even though both she and Stephie handled it well). It's too bad, since Mary Anne likes her so much, but that's the way things go.

As for me, I felt better about Carol. You might even have said I was feeling friendly towards her. Or at least friendlier. You'll see this as I tell you about our last (great!) day together in California. As I had written to my grandparents, we went to Magic Mountain, and then out for a really spectacular dinner.

This time, we didn't take any "extras" along on our trip, except for Carol, and Jeff. We were so excited about going to Magic Mountain! (Well, except for Mary Anne, who had read the brochure from cover to cover and was nervous about nearly every good ride.) At least she came along with us. I was afraid she might decide to stay at home.

"All those roller coasters!" She exclaimed that morning as we were getting dressed. Then she saw the rest of us packing our swimsuits. "What are those for?" she asked suspiciously.

"Water rides!" said Kristy gleefully.

Mary Anne looked so concerned that I couldn't help saying to her, "We can leave you in Bugs Bunny World, and you can go on the baby rides."

223

"I'm *not* a baby," Mary Anne replied indign-
antly.

"Come on, you lot. No fighting. It's our last
day here," said Claud.

So we stopped picking on Mary Anne, packed
up our things, climbed into the van, and were off.

"Ah, I just *love* amusement parks," said Jessi,
as we drove along. And when she first glimpsed
Magic Mountain, she shrieked, "There it is!"

Dad parked the van, we paid to go into the park
(Mal borrowed from Jessi), and . . .

"Oh, my lord! What should we do first?"
exclaimed Claud.

"The Tidal Wave!" shrieked Jeff, jumping up
and down. The Tidal Wave is a water ride
(obviously) and it's a new attraction at the park.
You go barrelling down this chute (in a roller
coaster car) and hit a twenty-foot wall of water,
which of course makes a huge, drenching splash.

"Let's save the water rides for later," said Dad,
but he was outvoted.

"We should do them first so we'll be dry by the
time we go to dinner," I pointed out sensibly.

"Okay," said Dad.

Off we went. We tore down the Tidal Wave
first. (Mary Anne wouldn't go.) Then we did the
Roaring Rapids, which is like shooting the rapids.
(Mary Anne decided that was safe, and actually
enjoyed herself.) After that, we tried the Log
Jammer, which Mary Anne informed us is the

longest water flume ride in the entire country. She put her foot down (and so did Dad) at the Jet Stream, though. That's another flume ride, but it ends with a 52-foot drop (according to Mary Anne's brochure). So Dad and Mary Anne drank lemonade and dried off while the rest of us braved the ride. At the end, I actually found myself grabbing Carol (even though she was sitting in front of me, and we were supposed to be holding on to the safety bar).

When the ride was over, Carol smiled at me and put her arm across my shoulders, but she didn't say anything about what had happened. I decided that Carol was a kid and an adult at the same time, and that was nice. She would do silly things with us, but she knew when to open her mouth and when not to.

After the water rides, we took a break for lunch (which made Stacey nervous because she was afraid that someone would get sick on the next ride, and Stacey can't *stand* to see anyone being sick.) But Stacey was safe. We went on *five* rides. (Well, some of us did. Mary Anne sat out on three of them.) And nobody was sick. Here's what we went on: a *gigantic* roller coaster called the Colossus; Freefall, which makes you feel weight-less; Ninja, the most incredible roller coaster I've ever been on; Revolution, on which you make a complete circle (in other words, you speed along upside down for a while); and finally Condor.

225

Now, the Condor is really something. It raises you away up in the air, spins you around, and you keep spinning until you touch the ground again.

At that point, we were all feeling rather shaken up, so we decided to leave the park. (Shaken up or not, we'd had a *great* time.) Then we drove to this place that Jeff and Dad and I love, called Medieval Times. You pretend the year is 1093 and that you are guests of a royal family. You eat at these tables surrounding an arena where you watch all this old-fashioned stuff like jousting and sorcery. And everyone wears crowns and eats *huge* meals.

Since there were so many of us, we had to split into groups, and I ended up sitting next to Carol. She and I cheered for the same knight in the jousting contest, and Carol let me eat her soup, since I didn't like some of the things we were served for dinner. (You don't have a choice about what to eat.)

When dinner was over, we were exhausted and drove home. On the way, though, I started thinking about something, and when we reached our house, I said, "Carol, can you stay for a second? I've got something for you."

I had decided to give Carol the letter in person.

Carol and I went into the family room and shut the door.

"Here," I said to Carol as we sat down. "This is for you."

226

Carol took the letter questioningly. Then she opened it and read it. When she had finished, she said, "Dawn, I want you to know that this means a lot to me. It really does."

"Well, everything I said is true."

I could tell Carol was really flattered, but she didn't make a big thing about it. She didn't cry or anything like that. We just hugged quickly, and then Carol said she was tired and should go. I felt relieved—and proud of myself.

Saturday

Dear Dad, Jeff, and Carol,

Well, here we are, back on the plane. Before our holiday, two weeks seemed like such a long time. Now it seems far too short. I can't believe our visit is over. Jeff, you'd better come to Stoneybrook soon!

The film they're showing on the flight today sounds really, really boring, so none of us rented headphones. We're just looking at our souvenirs and eating everything that's offered. Claudia has eaten about ten packets of peanuts, and now Stacey is afraid that Claud will be sick

Thank you again for the great holiday!

Love and Sunshine,
Dawn

The Schafers
and Carol Olson
22 Buena Vista

Palo City, Ca. 92800

23rd CHAPTER

Dawn

Our trip was almost over. A lot of goodbyes had been said (but a lot of hellos were yet to come). Last night, Claud and Terry said goodbye. Unfortunately they couldn't do this in person since we got back from the medieval feast quite late. They had to say goodbye over the phone.

Kristy, Stacey, Mary Anne, Jessi, Mal, and I wanted to listen in on Claud's end of the conversation, but we knew better. This was *really* personal. Besides, we knew Claud would tell us about the conversation (or at least about parts of it) when she got off the phone.

We were right.

Claud emerged from the den looking teary-eyed, so we surrounded her and moved into my room.

"What happened?" asked Stacey. She and Claud sat next to each other on my bed, and the rest of us draped ourselves around the room.

"Terry said he would miss me forever and never stop thinking of me," said Claud, wiping her eyes with the back of one hand.

I saw Jessi, Mal, and Mary Anne gape.

"That is *so* romantic." Mary Anne looked as if she were going to faint.

I thought of something then and tiptoed out of the room, leaving my friends to talk to Claud. I walked down the hall and knocked on Jeff's door.

"Yes?" he said. (I could see light under his door, so I knew he wasn't asleep yet. I hoped he would be in the mood for a talk.)

"It's Dawn. Can I come in?"

"Of course."

I opened the door to the absolute mess that Jeff calls his room. In most ways he's neat and tidy, but his room looks like a pigsty. However, Jeff swears it's an organized pigsty. "Quiz me," he'd said once. "Ask me where anything is and I can find it in five seconds."

Well, that was too good a challenge to turn down. "Your maths book," I said.

Jeff unearthed it from a pile of junk on the floor. "Four seconds!" he announced triumphantly.

I tried a few other things, and he beat his four-second record.

Anyway, I now picked my way through the stuff on Jeff's floor (which, by the way, Mrs Bruen is not allowed to move or even touch).

"Jeff?" I said. "I want to talk to you for a minute."

"Okay. What about? Am I in trouble?"

"No. I want to talk about Carol."

Jeff rolled his eyes.

"That's exactly what I mean," I said. "Neither of us has been very fair to Carol. We haven't given her a chance."

"Dawn, you don't live out here," said Jeff, as I tried to clear a spot for myself on his overflowing bed. "You've only seen her for two weeks. I see her almost every day."

"I know that. But in the two weeks, my feelings about her have changed. I started off disliking her, too." I tried to explain to Jeff how I'd thought Carol was trying to act like our friend or our big sister. "But when Stacey was in the car accident, I saw Carol completely differently. She really is an adult, Jeff."

"She's not our mother," he said, picking at a corner of his pillow.

"No. And she never will be. But if she and Dad get married, I think it will be okay. I really do."

Jeff just shrugged.

"All I'm saying is give her a chance, okay?"

Jeff paused. "Okay," he replied at last.

"Thanks . . . Jeffie," I said, using my baby name for him.

Jeff hit me over the head with his pillow, so I whacked him with a foam rubber baseball bat. Then, giggling, I fled his room.

The next morning, our household was up early, and Mrs Bruen arrived early, too. She prepared us a huge breakfast.

"Heaven knows what time they'll feed you on that plane . . . Or *what* they'll feed you. Eat up here, girls. I'll make whatever you want."

And she did. By the time we were leaving for the airport, we were stuffed.

Also, by the time we were leaving for the airport, Carol had arrived, and she came with us. By now I thought of her as one of the family. I would have been surprised if she *hadn't* come with us.

At the airport, there was the usual flurry of checking tickets and luggage. We had a lot more bags to check in than we'd had in New York. This was because some of us had bought an awful lot of souvenirs. Stacey, for instance had bought a gigantic Porky Pig somewhere. (Stacey can imitate Porky's voice perfectly.) And Terry had apparently given Claud a big present, although she wouldn't say what it was. (We suspected it was a stuffed animal.) Then there were Jessi and Mary

Anne. They had bought little things wherever we went: anything that said *California* or *Universal Studios* or *Magic Mountain* or whatever on it. They decided to check in some of these things and to bring others with them on the plane. (This turned out to be a good idea, since the film was so boring.)

At any rate, we were soon standing around our gate, waiting for our plane to be announced. We were excited and sad at the same time. We wanted to see our families again, but we weren't quite ready to say goodbye to California. And I wasn't ready to say goodbye to Dad or Jeff.

Or Carol.

But soon it was announced that boarding would begin.

My friends and I looked at each other. "I suppose this is it," said Jessi.

"Thank you, Mr Schafer," rose a chorus of voices.

Except for mine. I just put my arms around Dad and began to cry. "I don't want to leave you," I managed to say.

"I don't want you to leave me, either," he replied. "This is an awful way to live. But we've got to make the best of it. You know you'll be back again soon. You could even take a Friday and Monday off school and come out for a long weekend. Okay?"

"Okay."

Then I turned to Carol and gave her a quick hug. After that, I turned to Jeff. "No hugging," he whispered fiercely. "Not in public."

"All right." But I leaned over and whispered to him, "Remember what I said. Give Carol a chance."

Jeff nodded.

And a few minutes later, my friends and I were on the plane. We found our seats—seven across again—and settled in. Mary Anne immediately fastened her seat belt. Before she could tell the rest of us to do the same, we fastened them ourselves.

Z-O-O-O-O-M. We took off. Orange juice was served. The peanuts started coming around. We found out what the film was, rejected it, and got bored.

Then Jessi and Mary Anne started bringing out some of their souvenirs.

"Look!" said Jessi. She held up something like a back scratcher, but with an alligator's (a crocodile's?) head at one end. When you squeezed the other end, the mouth opened and closed.

"Now, what are you going to do with that?" Mal asked Jessi.

"Give it to you," Jessi replied. "It's a souvenir for you. You ought to have at least one from our trip."

Hours later (it seemed like days later), the plane

235

landed. The BSC members hurried out of their seats.

"Come on, you lot. We're here!" I cried.

We worked our way into the terminal as fast as we could without stampeding everybody, and suddenly—there were our families. Our parents and brothers and sisters and even some grandparents were there.

"Hello! Welcome back!" they cried.

I saw my mum and flew into her arms. "Oh, I missed you," I said.

"I missed you, too, darling."

We looked at each other with tears in our eyes. "It's so good to be home," I told her.

236

EPILOGUE

Dawn

DEAR MARY ANNE,

Hi! How ARE You? I AM FINE.
REALLY. DADDY SAID MAYBE I CAN
GET A POODLE. OH, GUESS WHAT.
A NEW FAMILY MOVED IN NEXT
DOOR. THERE'S A GIRL JUST MY
AGE IN IT. HER NAME IS MARGIE.
WE PLAY TOGETHER. MARGIE HAS
DRESSING - UP CLOTHES.
THANK YOU FOR YOUR LETTER.
LOVE,
STEPHIE

Dawn

Dear Terry,

Here is what I pormissed you. Its a picture of mimi, my grandmother I mean its a photoe of the portrit I pianted of her. now you can see mimi and my arturok.

Write now I am workig on a scluptue of a seagul. It is hard to make him look lick hes flying but Im doing my best. If it turns owt well i'll will send you a photoe.

Seen any good films lately?

I realy, realy, realy, realy, realy miss you.

xxx ooo

Sorry Sloppy   Claudia

Dear Claudia,

Thank You For Your Letter And The Photo. I can't Believe What A Good Artist You Are. Actually, I Can Believe It. I Just Wasn't Expecting Something So Sensational.

YES, I'VE SEEN THREE REALLY GOOD FILMS LATELY. I'VE GOT HOOKED ON WOODY ALLEN. USUALLY, I LIKE OLD FILMS, BUT WOODY ALLEN IS GREAT. I'VE SEEN <u>INTERIORS</u>, <u>ANNIE HALL</u> AND <u>LOVE AND DEATH</u>. TRY THEM SOMETIME.

DO YOU THINK YOU'LL BE IN CA AGAIN? I HOPE SO.

LOVE YOU FOREVER,
TERRY

Dear Dawn,

So how are things on the East Coast? We miss you! Everything here is cool. Stephie has a best friend! And she's got a dog. You'd better come and visit again soon. Say hi to Mary Anne, Jessi, Stacey, Kristy, Mallory, and Claudia.

Love,
The We ♥ Kids Club

Dawn

Dear Carol,
    I **really** miss California,
especially Jeff and Dad. I miss
you, too. But I'm glad to be
back in Stoneybrook. It's funny,
but I don't know which place
to call home. Right now, I
sort of think of both places
as home.
    Will you write to me?
                Sincerely,
                Dawn

Dear Dawn,
    Of course I'll write to you!
How are you? How is school
going? How is the Babysitters
Club?
    I think you can consider
both California and Connecticut
home. That's nice — Not
too many people can have real
homes on both sides of the
country.

240

I'd like to talk to you on the phone, and I'm sure I will soon.

Love,
Carol

P.S. Jeff says hi

So that's our story. Did you ever think that a lottery ticket could cause all this—a journey, a boyfriend, surfing, dyed hair . . .

By the way, we did a *great* job choosing Mallory's hair colour. We've been home for a month now, so of course her hair is growing out, and you can't see the difference at all. Here's what Mal has to say about this: *Whew!*

Well, the Jack-O'-Lottery has reached another all-time high. At the next BSC meeting, I'm going to suggest chipping in and buying seven more tickets. They say lightning never strikes twice in the same place, but who knows? If we won, maybe we could all go to New York and stay at Stacey's father's apartment!

241

GREEN WATCH by Anthony Masters

GREEN WATCH is a new series of fast moving environmental thrillers, in which a group of young people battle against the odds to save the natural world from ruthless exploitation. All titles are printed on recycled paper.

BATTLE FOR THE BADGERS
Tim's been sent to stay with his weird Uncle Seb and his two kids, Flower and Brian, who run Green Watch – an environmental pressure group. At first Tim thinks they're a bunch of cranks – but soon he finds himself battling to save badgers from extermination . . .

SAD SONG OF THE WHALE
Tim leaps at the chance to join Green Watch on an anti-whaling expedition. But soon, he and the other members of Green Watch, find themselves shipwrecked and fighting for their lives . . .

DOLPHIN'S REVENGE
The members of Green Watch are convinced that Sam Jefferson is mistreating his dolphins – but how can they prove it? Not only that, but they must save Loner, a wild dolphin, from captivity . . .

MONSTERS ON THE BEACH
The Green Watch team is called to investigate a suspected radiation leak. Teddy McCormack claims to have seen mutated crabs and sea-plants, but there's no proof, and Green Watch don't know whether he's crazy or there's been a cover-up . . .

GORILLA MOUNTAIN
Tim, Brian and Flower fly to Africa to meet the Bests, who are protecting gorillas from poachers. But they are ambushed and Alison Best is kidnapped. It is up to them to rescue her *and* save the gorillas . . .

SPIRIT OF THE CONDOR
Green Watch has gone to California on a surfing holiday – but not for long! Someone is trying to kill the Californian Condor, the bird cherished by an Indian tribe – the Daiku – without which the tribe will die. Green Watch must struggle to save both the Condor and the Daiku . . .

POINT HORROR

Introducing a new series of horror fiction for young adults
– read them if you dare!

APRIL FOOLS by Richie Tankersley Cusick
Driving back from a party on April 1st Belinda, Frank and
Hildy are involved in a gruesome accident. Thinking no
one could have survived, they run away from the scene.
But someone must have survived the crash, and they're
going to make Belinda suffer for what happened . . .

TRICK OR TREAT by Richie Tankersley Cusick
From the beginning Martha knew there was something
evil about the house; something cold; something sinister.
Then the practical jokes begin, and she is sure someone is
following her . . .

MY SECRET ADMIRER by Carol Ellis
Jenny's parents go away leaving her alone in their new
house. Then the phonecalls start – Jenny has a secret
admirer who courts her with sweet messages, but she also
has an enemy who chases her on a lonely road. She has no
one to turn to except her secret admirer – but who is he? . . .

THE LIFEGUARD by Richie Tankersley Cusick
Kelsey's summer on Beverley Island should have been
paradise, but it quickly turns into a nightmare. It starts
with a message from a girl who's missing, and there have
been a number of suspicious drownings. At least the
lifeguards will protect her. Poor Kelsey. Someone forgot to
tell her that lifeguards don't always like to save lives . . .

BEACH PARTY by R.L. Stine
Karen plans to party all summer with her friend Ann-Marie. The fun starts when she meets two new guys. But which should she choose: handsome Jerry or dangerous Vince? But the party turns nasty when the threats start. Someone wants Karen to stay away from Jerry at all costs . . .

FUNHOUSE by Diane Hoh
Everyone in Santa Luisa is horrified when the Devil Elbow's roller coaster flies off its rails. And no one believes Tess when she says she saw someone tampering with the track. But someone knows Tess is telling the truth – someone who is playing a deadly game, and Tess is in the way . . .

THE BABY-SITTER by R.L. Stine
From the moment that Jenny accepts the Hagen baby-sitting job, she knows she's made a terrible mistake. The Hagen house fills her with horror, and she finds a creepy "neighbour" prowling in the back yard. Then the crank phonecalls start – but who wants to hurt her? What kind of maniac is willing to scare her . . . to death? . . .

Look out for:
Teacher's Pet by Richie Tankersley Cusick
The Boyfriend by R.L. Stine

THE BABYSITTERS CLUB

Need a babysitter? Then call the Babysitters Club. Kristy Thomas and her friends are all experienced sitters. They can tackle any job from rampaging toddlers to a pandemonium of pets. To find out all about them, read on!

Look out for:

The Babysitters Club No 15:
Little Miss Stoneybrook . . . and Dawn
The Babysitters Club No 16:
Jessi's Secret Language
The Babysitters Club No 17:
Mary Anne's Bad Luck Mystery
The Babysitters Club No 18:
Stacey's Mistake
The Babysitters Club No 19:
Claudia and the Bad Joke
The Babysitters Club No 20:
Kristy and the Walking Disaster
The Babysitters Club No 21:
Mallory and the Trouble with Twins
The Babysitters Club No 22:
Jessi Ramsey, Pet-sitter
The Babysitters Club No 23:
Dawn on the Coast
The Babysitters Club No 24:
Kristy and the Mother's Day Surprise

You'll find these and many more fun Hippo books at your
local bookseller, or you can order them direct. Just send off
to Customer Services, Hippo Books, Westfield Road,
Southam, Leamington Spa, Warwickshire CV33 0JH, not
forgetting to enclose a cheque or postal order for the price
of the book(s) plus 30p per book for postage and packing.

MYSTERY THRILLERS

Introducing a new series of hard-hitting action-packed thrillers for young adults.

THE SONG OF THE DEAD by Anthony Masters
For the first time in years "the song of the dead" is heard around Whitstable. Is it really the cries of dead sailors? Or is it something more sinister? Barney Hampton is determined to get to the bottom of the mystery . . .

THE FERRYMAN'S SON by Ian Strachan
Rob is convinced that Drewe and Miles are up to no good. Where do they go on their night cruises? And why does Kimberley go with them? When Kimberley disappears Rob finds himself embroiled in a web of deadly intrigue . . .

TREASURE OF GREY MANOR by Terry Deary
When Jamie Williams and Trish Grey join forces for a school history project, they unearth much more than they bargain for! The diary of the long-dead Marie Grey hints at the existence of hidden treasure. But Jamie and Trish aren't the only ones interested in the treasure – and some people don't mind playing dirty . . .

THE FOGGIEST by Dave Belbin
As Rachel and Matt Gunn move into their new home, a strange fog descends over the country. Then Rachel and Matt's father disappears from his job at the weather station, and they discover the sinister truth behind the fog . . .

BLUE MURDER by Jay Kelso
One foggy night Mack McBride is walking along the pier when he hears a scream and a splash. Convinced that a murder has been committed he decides to investigate and finds himself in more trouble than he ever dreamed of . . .

DEAD MAN'S SECRET by Linda Allen
After Annabel's Uncle Nick is killed in a rock-climbing accident, she becomes caught up in a nerve-wracking chain of events. Helped by her friends Simon and Julie, she discovers Uncle Nick was involved in some very unscrupulous activities . . .

CROSSFIRE by Peter Beere
After running away from Southern Ireland Maggie finds herself roaming the streets of London destitute and alone. To make matters worse, her step-father is an important member of the IRA – if he doesn't find her before his enemies do, she might just find herself caught up in the crossfire . . .

THE THIRD DRAGON by Garry Kilworth
Following the massacre at Tiananmen Square Xu flees to Hong Kong, where he is befriended by John Tenniel, and his two friends Peter and Jenny. They hide him in a hillside cave, but soon find themselves swept up in a hazardous adventure that could have deadly results . . .

VANISHING POINT by Anthony Masters
In a strange dream, Danny sees his father's train vanishing into a tunnel, never to be seen again. When Danny's father really does disappear, Danny and his friend Laura are drawn into a criminal world, far more deadly than they could ever have imagined . . .